The Elves of Christmas

By

Wendy Rathbone

Eye Scry Publications

Chapter One

"Santa is coming! Santa is coming!" The cries rang throughout the workshop. Elves ran up and down the golden halls.

I caught sight of Bell, Ever and Clove coming in from the snowy landscape, long hair white with crystal flakes.

"How long do we have?" I asked, looking up from my line of dolls whose eyes I had just finished painting.

Jingle came into view. "Word came in minutes ago. He's coming tomorrow morning. We have less than 24 hours."

Tinsel yelled, "I need help in the kitchens. Volunteers, please?" He was our best chef. "Peppermint cake with butter cream frosting. And sugar cookies. And donuts stuffed with whipped cream. They're his favorites! Oh gods, I don't have enough time."

This would be a long night. We would all be staying up to get ready.

Jingle, who was our boss, said, "Pepper, make sure all the windows are clean."

I hated washing windows, but I said nothing since I was ahead of schedule with my chores and would be expected to do extra. Besides, it was for Santa. All of us would do anything for that guy. He really was the jolliest, most generous, and charismatic elf who ever lived. Everyone loved him. In a way, he was like our king, ruler of Santa's Village where all who worked for him lived at the North Pole.

Jingle told me most people who believe in Santa Claus also think his elves are diminutive beings from a magical realm. He blamed it on Hollywood, and before that it was the fault of the publishing industry that cranked out funny children's books for the winter holidays.

The truth is we elves were all different: short, tall, round, thin, blond, brunet, pale gold, dark brown. We look a lot like humans, except we aren't.

I have small, pointed ears, a compact, muscular body, and what Jingle says is a "broody dark complexion." Thus, my name sort of fits me. Pepper.

Jingle, on the other hand, has large ears due to being over one hundred years old, and a jolly round belly he emphasizes with pride by wearing big leather belts decorated with square pouches, a drink cup holder, and hanging trinkets (ornaments and crystals he likes to collect).

Centuries ago, our race came from a parallel Earth which was destroyed by a comet. We fled destruction through dimensional portals to this current Earth. We chose to stay apart from humans, invisible to them, and remained in the north. We had gold enough for all our needs, and imported food and fuel from many countries, but there wasn't much to do in such cold climate, so we turned to making things.

When I was new to the workshop in the North Pole, Jingle took me under his wing. I had been such a nervous newbie. I hero-worshipped Santa. As an artist, I had wanted to work for him for such a long time. When I was finally chosen, my initial ecstasy turned to outright terror. What if I wasn't good enough? What if Santa hated me? What if I was fired from my first job and sent to do non-creative work such as stable-mucking or, worse, finance?

But everything turned out just fine. I am an excellent toy designer with original ideas. I create the most beautiful rocking horses and dolls you'll ever see.

Blizzard season had not yet scented the air. It was still October but the sun was already setting earlier every day, and coming up late. Because there had been few storms, the windows were not too bad.

I headed to the main kitchen to begin filling buckets with water for the task when I heard Jingle say, "Ice, you help Pepper with the windows."

My stomach froze. I turned, frowning. Jingle knew I did not interact with Ice. I kept my distance from him. Ice worked in the electronics department. Our lines of work never crossed, thankfully. But Ice must've come into the front rooms to see what was going on. And Jingle was putting any elf passing by to work.

Like me, Ice fit his name well. His long, tall body and pale skin made him look as if he was carved from frozen tundra. He had white blond hair that hung to his ass, cold blue eyes and what seemed to be a permanent smirk. I confess I initially did not like him because of that sneer, and because he hung with a more irreverent crowd, some of whom had been known to talk shit about Santa and this new Earth and how kids were so privileged these days they didn't appreciate the presents we made anymore.

My workmate, Pumpkin, whined, "This is so unfair! Santa needs to give us notice. Just to pop in like this. It's freaking me out."

"Get hold of yourself," I said. Then I leaned forward and said in a whisper, "Look, I have to work with Ice. None of this is fair."

He pouted, his red hair sparkling with the bit of glitter he'd made a mess of while trying to finish up a line of necklaces netted with little bottles labeled "Fairy Dust."

"But Ice likes you, even if you don't like him," Pumpkin muttered.

"What? He does not." Frowning, I turned to look at Ice, who was glaring at me as if he couldn't start on the windows without me. He was far enough away that he couldn't hear us.

"What makes you say that anyway?" I asked Pumpkin.

He shrugged. "Everyone knows."

"How?"

"Whenever he's around, he stares at you."

"He glares like he's doing now," I argued. "Once when I glared back, he told me to fuck off. And you know me, I get along with everyone."

Pumpkin shrugged. "It's just what people are saying."

"Well, people are wrong." I turned away.

I moved toward Ice and the kitchen. He seemed to be glowering now. I ignored it, moved alongside him and said, "We'll start in the north wing and move along east. Then we'll do the upstairs."

"I'm not going to do anything you say," he muttered.

"Fine. Suit yourself." I turned my back on him. I had always been put off by his surly attitude. I could not figure out why Santa had chosen him to work in the toy shop. But for his beauty—and he was an uncommonly handsome elf—he always seemed so bitter, angry, even resentful. Every other elf I'd ever known had been honored to be one of Santa's chosen.

I started filling two wooden buckets with hot water and soap. A mint scent wafted up. We could have used spray soap and cotton cloths, but to clean that way left a film on the glass. For Santa, we all wanted to look our best. The windows would gleam in the starlight with my mixture of soap, water and squeegee.

Ice took up one of the buckets without my having to ask. I noticed the flex of his arm muscles as he did so, and the way his long hair fell forward, chiming because of little bells he'd attached to random, skinny braids hiding in the flaxen silks of his locks. For a single instant I thought about how it might feel to touch those locks. Probably like cashmere in their softness, but cool like satin.

6

I looked away quickly, my cheeks heating. What was I thinking? I disliked Ice in every way.

Though he had made a big deal out of not doing what I said, he followed me, wordless, to the north wing. We each started on a paned window, side by side. Sponging the soapy liquid on the glass, I drew the rubber squeegee edge down to clean it.

Santa's Village resided in the depths of the northern ice, its lanes and avenues stretching from the center, like a snowflake. The workshop occupied the outskirts of Santa's Village, and the view outside led to ice cliffs of pink, blue and mauve in the undulating, seemingly perpetual duskiness of October. It looked as if the snow and ice had once been a white sea that had been flash-frozen that way. The shining wall below the precipice contained an inner light, a soul pulsing with life yet to be released.

On the horizon, the greenish sky rose up to brushstrokes of flamingo pink. At its zenith, the blue there was of such a deep shade it made the breath catch in my throat. It always made me think of vastness. Of how small I was in the scope of universal rhythms. It was still too early for starlight, but the cliff-snow sparkled like stars fallen long ago from a distance too great to fathom.

I never tired of the beauty of the north. Or the cold. Or even the isolation. It filled me up inside even while making me feel insignificant. The combination of those feelings gave me a longing I took pleasure from, a yearning I could not quite put a definition to. And always, inside the workshop, I had warmth, burning hearths, friends, and cocoa to look forward to every day.

"You're dripping." Ice's sulky tone interrupted my reverie.

I looked to see the puddle I'd made on the shiny, wood floor. I'd been daydreaming. I hadn't even noticed.

He laughed when I bent to clean the little pool of liquid.

7

"Thinking of Santa?" he quipped.

"No."

"Not like all the others, then? Smitten. In love."

"What?" I turned to look at him.

He faced the window, finishing up. It looked perfect, scintillating from refracted ice-light.

"Santa has many lovers. Don't you want to be one of them?"

"What? No. I can't believe-- What are you saying?" I'd never thought of Santa that way. He was more of a father figure to me. And old. Very old. He was my hero. I became tongue-tied around him. I wanted to please him, but not erotically.

He did not answer my sputtering questions. Instead, he let out a quiet hiss and moved on to the next window, pushing the plaid fleece curtains aside and affixing them with a red ribbon.

In his white sleeveless shirt that fastened like a wrap about his slim waist, he looked over-dressed for doing such a small task. His trousers were black, and made of expensive wool. I could tell because they were smooth but still looked warm, not like my ratty sweats. We both wore curl-toed shoes, but his were polished to a shine that glistened. Mine were years old.

We were paid a good salary in our jobs, but I didn't waste mine on imported clothes. I saved almost every penny—for what, I did not know—for I needed nothing. Food and board were provided. But Ice, well, Ice—he must've spent every penny he earned on things to wear. Like the bells in his hair, which looked to be pure sterling. And in his earlobes and on every finger flashed a ring; all the metals looked like platinum to match his cold spirit.

Now Ice wetted his squeegee again, dipping his hands in warm water as if not noticing—or caring—that his pretty rings got soaked.

I finished my window minutes later and moved on to the one on his other side.

8

I had on a lightweight gray sweater and my sleeves were getting wet as I kept dripping water. As the air dried them a little, my skin prickled with cold.

Silence overwhelmed us. All I could hear was a crackling of the hearth at the end of the chamber. Where we were was called a long-room, a recreational area filled with plush chairs and couches where elves could take breaks between the long work hours. There were round tables for playing cards, or doing puzzles. A flat-screen TV filled one wall. But the outer wall was almost all windows. The architects of the shop had designed this room around the view.

It was a lovely place to relax, one of my favorites other than my own chair in front of the fire in my own small cabin.

Ice gave a little chuckle again, as if he was still thinking of our last short conversation.

I couldn't keep my mouth shut. "You are so disparaging. Is it Santa you particularly don't like, or just all of us?"

"Fuck off," was all I got in reply.

I could not figure him out. But it wasn't my job to fix others. Only toys. Toys were my element.

But I kept wondering about him. He didn't seem to want to be here, so why had he been chosen by Santa? I'd heard only rumors about his past since he'd arrived last year. One speculation said he used to work in the stables and was on duty the night Dasher disappeared. Dasher had been one of Santa's oldest and most beloved reindeer. He'd since been replaced by Dasher2. But honestly, Ice did not seem to be the "stable boy" type, and Pumpkin, who loved to gossip, told me the rumors were false.

Another rumor said he was really a human disguised as an elf, infiltrating our secret abode and reporting back to the FBI. That had mostly been a joke told at a late-night party where we'd all had too much eggnog.

Pretty much, I figured Ice was good at what he did in the electronics department, liked the work, and that was it. Also, a job in Santa's Village came with complete benefits, private cabins, meals, and bosses like Jingle who never raised his voice. Who could say no to that?

The two elves I often saw Ice hanging out with were Syl and North. Syl might have fit the diminutive definition of the Hollywood elf, she was so petite, but we all learned quickly not to make assumptions based on her looks.

Her every other word was an expletive. She might wear red dresses and decorate her hair with tinsel, but when her eyebrows came together in flares of anger, you knew not to test her. She spoke always in a loud voice. She disapproved of everything. But her talent could not be denied. She was a fantastic actress, and was the voice of hundreds of automated, talking toys.

She and Ice weren't lovers. They were just a good match, a shared negativity feeding arrogance that seemed to entertain them. North was actually Syl's lover. He had short black hair trained into spikes. He rarely spoke, but he followed Syl and Ice everywhere, almost as if he were on a leash.

I finished my second window and moved on to a third. Ice had already done four, and they shimmered without streaks.

Closer to the fire now, I could smell the imported, flaming oak. Crumbs of wood and ash scattered across the exterior of the hearth, and needed to be cleaned. I made a mental note to get to that after the windows.

Normally, I enjoyed the silences of life, of still snow, fire-lit rooms, bedrooms filled with books. But this silence between me and Ice had become a burning thing between us. As if all consciousness were focused on it, which made it an effort, which made it bigger than it should be.

I kept feeling as if he was staring at me. But when I would turn, he would be quietly working as if nothing were out of the ordinary.

I tried to focus on anything but the silence. But all I heard were the little ringing bells in his hair when he moved, and the shuffle of his feet. I thought I could even hear him breathe. In this silence, which was induced by him, all I could hear was him.

A heat built in the bottom of my stomach, like a sort of untapped rage. I suddenly wanted him to stop being in the room with me, stop washing the windows, stop not talking. It was making me frustrated beyond my usual easy demeanor.

I placed my squeegee in the bucket. The warm water sloshed, droplets like diamonds landing on my curled shoes. I turned to face him. The fire warmed against my back like a fever, but my body was strangely chilled.

He stood by the largest picture window furthest from the hearth, white on white, his body, hair, shirt, and the snow outside all melting together. He was framed by dimness, pink and blue and soft. The gold of the interior ceiling lights raced and met in his hair.

An oval, hand-woven Nordic rug of maroon and beige, like a piece of softly curled candy, lay in front of me. I stepped onto it, hands gripped at my sides, watching him. It took me too long to realize he could see me in his window's reflection.

Though he said nothing, I was suddenly mortified.

"I can finish in here. You can go." My words were so abrupt, they surprised even me. But the thought of him being gone was irresistibly comforting.

He kept polishing the window with a bit of soft, blue cloth. The glass was already dry.

"No," he said, without turning.

Just that one single word.

My fingers clenched tighter, my nails poking my palms. I didn't know what to do. Or say.

I looked right and then left. We had two more windows to do before we were done.

Finally, he spoke again, a soft mutter. "If you don't like me here, too bad. Jingle said we had to work together."

My mind wanted to defend against his words. But he was right. I didn't like him in the room. I'd just asked him to leave. But all my life, even when I didn't like another elf, I had never been outright rude. What was wrong with me?

"Fine," I heard myself say. I almost didn't recognize my voice.

"Fine," he echoed.

At last he turned, his thin, snowy brows frowning. "And I already told you, I'm not doing anything you say."

"I didn't say you should," I shot back.

"You fancied yourself my boss from the moment we were given this assignment."

"I didn't." Did I? I thought back on my actions. I had only asked him to come with me. I hadn't thought I was being bossy.

"Well, my only boss is Jingle," he said, and tossed his head back as if even admitting that was toxic to him.

"And Santa," I added.

He let out a disgusted noise. It sounded like, "Tuh!"

"Gods, why do you hate him so much?"

"None of your business," he retorted.

"But he's Santa. He's wonderful."

Now he looked hard and unbending, his body stiff and possibly even taller as he stood back, head up, eyes on nothing in particular. The bells in his braids went silent. He crossed his bare arms, the blue cloth crumpled in one tight fist. "I'm sure he is."

I nodded. "He is. It's a certainty."

"Yeah, well, that has nothing to do with me."

Such an odd response. My mind could not make sense of him at all.

12

"Santa is why we're here," I said.

He lowered his head, looked me up, then down. "You, maybe."

"What, do you owe some debt to Santa, or something? Are you here against your will?"

The air came out of his lungs almost like a hiss. He turned back toward the window. "Let's just get this done. The hearth needs cleaning, too."

I bristled. Defensive again. "I already noticed."

Trying not to grumble under my breath, I took up the broom and dust pan.

From across the room, little bells pinged in a light and scintillating tone. I tried not to hear them.

Chapter Two

Ice and I took time out for a quick toasted cheese sandwich. In the dining hall, I noticed Ice looking for his friends. But they were nowhere about. Two other elves, Garland and Startree, sat chatting in one corner over cocoa, but as we came in they left immediately to go back to work.

The area was quiet. Most of the elves were frantically working, taking few or no breaks. Our own reprieve would have been considered luxurious in this moment. But after we cleaned two room's worth of windows and hearths, Ice complained he was starving.

We were not allowed in the kitchen proper. Tinsel had all the ovens and burners going in there, and a dozen elves as his assistants. The place was crazy.

But there was a small hotplate in the corner of the dining hall. I made two sandwiches and handed one to Ice. It wasn't like I was doing him a favor. It was just easier to make two at once than toast them back to back.

He took his time getting his coffee. When he approached my table he acted quite reluctant to sit with me, and I pretended not to care. But in the end, he sat two chairs down from me at the same table, setting his steaming coffee in front of him and his plate to the side. He poured a waterfall of sugar into his cup, slowly stirring. Like most elves, he was a sweetoholic. I noticed he took no cream.

I took a bite of my toasted cheese. There is no better comfort food, I'm convinced. I felt my body go into a kind of languid state, relishing the taste.

"It's good."

I looked up. Was Ice giving me a compliment? But he hadn't even taken a bite. He was still fiddling with his coffee.

"My specialty," I replied.

I kept eating. But I watched him out the corner of my eye as he took the sandwich in his glittery, be-ringed hands and raised it to his lips. When he opened his mouth, his pink lips surrounded the corner of the sandwich, curved about it and bit. He pulled the sandwich away and some cheese stretched, then broke.

He ate so delicately for one so crabby. I held back a smile. Also, just the thought that it was a sandwich I had made that he was eating made a spark of pride settle in my chest. His jaw undulated. His high cheekbones moved as he chewed. Damn, but he was lovely.

I didn't want to be thinking this, so I took another bite of my own sandwich and focused on its soft toasted crunch, the buttery flavor, the tender texture of the cheese. It would do no good for me to be thinking of anything else today. I had no time. Santa was coming.

We finished without speaking and took our dishes to the washer.

Grabbing our buckets and filling them with fresh hot water, we gave the kitchen windows a quick wash, dodging busy elf bakers, then the front room where Santa would be received. The hearth there was clean.

Then we moved on to a small parlor and some offices. It was all quick work.

The upper levels of the workshop—both the second and third floor—held large rooms in various states of disarray. Each work-room focused on a specialty. Elves were busily cleaning rugs, hearths, tables, clutter. The pinewood walls were gleaming, the floors freshly waxed. Some elves were putting finishing touches on new products to show off to Santa. They did not even seem to notice us.

Jingle was in and out, giving kind orders in his soft voice, his large body practically dancing as he moved from room to room.

In the electronics room, Ice met up with Syl and North. I stood behind him, holding my bucket, suddenly intimidated. I'd avoided this group for so long. I didn't know them. I never thought I'd want to know them. They were louder than I preferred. They drank too much eggnog and spiked cider. They were irreverent.

"I'll just get these two windows," I said to Ice, not looking at him, not waiting for a response.

Of course I did not get one. He put his bucket down, the water sloshing almost over the sides, and North and Syl gathered on either side of him like black and scarlet shadows to show him something they were finishing up.

I heard some chuckles. Then I heard Syl say, rather loud, "Bullshit. You have the most talent!" More murmuring. North half-whispered, "You don't need his approval." I heard the word "Santa" a few times. Then I heard North hiss, "Fuck the windows. Finish the game."

"No," said Ice with a settled quietude I had not expected. "Jingle teamed me with Pepper. I have to finish the cleaning."

A tingle of surprise went down my spine when I heard my name. I didn't even think the others knew my name. None of us had ever made any effort to speak with one another. Plus, their off-putting vibe as a group had me and other elves avoiding them.

"Doing windows." Syl's brusque tone was softened by her wide smile. "How low you've sunk."

Ice shrugged. "My lot in life."

As other elves scurried frantically about the noisy, beeping room, Ice took up his bucket. I watched in my own window's reflection as he went to work, his beautiful friends staring after him with amused expressions on their faces.

I suddenly wondered, even though Syl and North were married, if the three were a triad. It was common for elves to form family groups of threes, to take two husbands or two wives, or one of each. But their body language did not communicate a sensual intimacy, but more a raucous and creative friendship with Ice.

My window faced the edge of the village this time, and all the lights were on. The site glimmered in my vision, the lanterns gold and red and green. Rows of little cabins, one of which was mine, sat in lovely little swirls of frosted snow. Their rooftops reflected the pink-green-blue sky.

From here on the second floor, I could see part of the snowflake design of the village, its multiple arms stretched in different directions and little areas of cabins clustered as end-points to each row. The center housed stables and stores. With everything lit up, the part of the giant snowflake I could see scintillated like a multi-colored crystal.

In the distance stood an ice castle looming out of the misty whiteness. A snow-cloud with turrets and peaked roofs. Santa's castle.

Though it was carved entirely of solid ice with an element that guaranteed it would never melt, even in the fiercest global warming summertime, the interior was warm and cozy.

I'd only been in two rooms, the front room and Santa's office. I had the fortune to meet Santa in his own home the day I was formally hired. He greeted every new elf that came to work for him in the workshop, but not always in his home. While I was there, I saw glowing crystal hearths dancing with orange flames in both rooms, their diamond-clear mantles decorated with pine and holly. Thick rugs of deepest reds lapped the white floor. Lanterns with paned windows gave off a honeyed light. Everything in that castle seemed as if it came from a dream.

Contrary to popular human culture, there was no Mrs. Claus. Santa had never married. But he had plenty of lovers. Of both genders. Some lived with him for many years, off and on. We elves gossiped about it, but most of us were discrete. Some elves longed to be his lovers. But not me. He was too intimidating! Besides, no one I personally knew had ever made it that far.

I thought again of Ice and his negative attitude. It couldn't be that something had happened between him and Santa. No. I could not believe it. He was too young, for one thing. But with elves who lived to be hundreds of years old, who could really know what was deemed too young? Too old?

I glanced over my shoulder. Ice was reaching up to squeegee the window, his long, lean frame stretched to full height. His chiming hair brushed his ass, reflecting all the white and gold tones of the room and the view outside. Damn. His beauty could shatter mirrors. But he seemed oblivious.

Just then, a small red minx of an elf came up behind me. "Pepper? Is that your name?"

I turned to look down at Syl. She was quite small. Her red dress was trimmed in faux white fur. She'd never paid a single moment of attention to me, not even when I'd been cleaning windows in electronics less than an hour ago.

"Yeah?"

She looked me up and down real slow, and I felt myself start to back up. She threw her head back, almost glowering. "Just checking." Then she sauntered away.

It was very strange.

I saw Ice watching. All I could do was shrug.

He turned away and finished his window.

When we were done with our chores, we went to Jingle for more orders.

"Good job," Jingle said. "I wish you could do the outsides, too, but that requires scaffolding and there's just no time. So it will have to do. At least you got the build up of smoke and dust off from the inside."

Ice stood to the side, looking bored. I remained attentive. I liked Jingle. Like Santa, he deserved all of my respect.

"Now," Jingle began, "I want decorations. Tasteful, not ostentatious, you hear me?"

I nodded. Ice shrugged one shoulder. Jingle didn't say one word to him about it. He was kind that way.

"And maybe a snowman or two outside along the front path."

I couldn't help but smile. I loved building snowmen.

"We're on it," I said.

It was already past dinnertime. We were going to be at this most of the night.

When Jingle left us, I turned to Ice. His pale blue eyes met mine. There was a hesitance there. An uneasiness. It made me feel uncomfortable with him all over again. But I pushed down my resentment of him and said, "Okay, where do you want to start first?"

"I don't care. Work is work," he replied.

"I love building snowmen."

He shook his head. "All right, then."

We bundled up in woolen scarves and bright green parkas. My mittens were green. Ice's were white. We both wore red and white striped knit caps with long

18

tops that hung to the center of our backs. Ice tucked his hair inside the back of his parka. No more chimes for a while.

No one could walk through soft snow in the perpetually sparkling dusk of a North Pole October and not be a little affected. I skipped a bit off the path, sinking knee deep, and couldn't help but grin.

Ice was more stoic, but I did notice a slight curve to his pale pink lips. He carried our snowman accessories, brooms, black hats, carrots, lumps of coal. He dumped them all in a pile, then turned full circle looking around.

"Why don't we make the first one right there?" he said, pointing at a red-striped light post.

"All right," I said. I couldn't tell if he was being a little friendlier, or just wanted to get things done as quickly as possible and be rid of me.

We began to pile snow to roll for the body of our ice sculpture being. Our breaths steamed the air. It was exhilarating.

As I worked, I decided to try to pull him into conversation. "I love the northern autumns. What about you?"

He looked at me strangely, but answered. "They're all right."

His reply was better than nothing.

We worked for some minutes in silence as I tried to think of something more to say. It wasn't easy, this feeling. Almost like being out of control. Not knowing what to say. Fearing his cold, strange tempers. It was stupid of me, I knew. Why should I care what Ice thought of me? I barely knew him.

Just as we were almost finished with the base of the snowman, I slipped. Snow went flying. I fell back into soft powder and lost my cap. The sky was dark blue now, and I saw one small star peeping out at me.

Then I saw white. I blinked. Ice was looking down at me with a perplexed gaze. His pale eyes seared into me, and I was instantly embarrassed.

"I'm all right," I said grumpily. But when I tried to get my feet underneath me, I slipped a little, and felt a small needle of pain in my knee. "Ow."

I thought I heard Ice sigh, but his next gesture belied it. He held out his hand to me. I couldn't believe it. For a guy who told me early on to "fuck off", this concern was new, and strange.

I did need the help, so I took his hand. He was quite gentle in pulling me up. He didn't even smirk. "Do you want to go in?" he asked.

"No, I'm fine. Just pulled a muscle in my knee, that's all."

"The cold won't be good for that."

"No, let's finish. I want to finish. I love making snowmen."

"Like your dolls."

I frowned, thinking he meant it as a tease. But his face was relaxed, not grimacing, not showing his core of displeasure at everything around him as he normally did.

"Yes," I finally said. "Kind of like that."

"Your dolls are works of art." He made the statement as if he were talking about the weather.

All I could think to say was, "Thank you."

"How long does it take to design one?"

He'd never asked me a question before.

"Days," I said. "Sometimes weeks."

"I like the one with the rainbow hair and the moth wing cape," he said.

"Darcy." I was stunned. I had had no clue he'd ever noticed my dolls, or even knew doll-making was my gift.

"You name them?" he asked.

I nodded. Were we actually having a conversation? About dolls? I almost couldn't breathe. I wanted to talk more, tell him everything about what it was like to design them, to draw the faces, make the clothes, make tiny doll jewelry, style the hair. But I didn't dare. He was skittish. I didn't want to push.

I said, "What you do in electronics is beyond my brain capacity. The players, the games, the consoles."

"Yes, but you're an artist. I'm just a tech." He bent over and began piling more snow.

"That's not true." I knew he created stories for games, not just the hardware. And he drew and painted his ideas as well. I'd seen still photo previews of his newest game, *Vampire Crusade*. It had gorgeous colors, the art like watercolors flowing into gothic backgrounds, the characters' capes and long hair mingling.

I moved to help with the main part of the snow body. My knee ached, but it was not too bad.

Ice's lips pressed tight. He kept working and would not look at me. Closed off again.

We finally got the body done and started putting on the accessories. I began to carve a friendly, smiling face with a spoon I'd pocketed from the dining hall. The carrot nose made him look silly, but I could at least give him cheeks, a chin, a forehead.

Ice put the coal in for the eyes and the mouth. He stuck a broom alongside the body, and pressed a mitten on either side for hands.

We stood back and assessed our sculpture. It was a traditional look, common. We looked at each other, a wordless expression of disappointment between us.

I said, "We can do better."

He nodded. And I thought I saw the hint of his smile again. Beautiful.

As we worked, my knee kept up its dim throb. Nothing serious, but I was mad that I got hurt at such a simple job.

Our second snowman became a real sculpture. Ice and I traded off with the spoon, but mostly we used our hands, mittens off, rubbing the feeling back into them every few minutes, and before we knew it a fairy-angel stood before us with swooping wings, a gentle face, arms folded before her. We did not use the coal or carrot or hat. She was just a white creature of the north, her own person of crystal ice and snow.

"Santa will be well-pleased," I said with a smile. As soon as I spoke, I wanted to take back the words.

A glower came over Ice. He hunched his shoulders under his parka. Closed in on himself. But he said nothing.

"All right then," I said, grabbing my mittens. "I guess we should go back inside."

Ice grunted, "Yeah." His voice came out monotone.

And then I saw it. He didn't really want to leave. He'd actually enjoyed himself. Building. Making something new and pretty.

As we walked up to the front door, me limping just a little, all the string lights were on, framing the windows and door, curling up the porch posts.

Some elf had changed the wreath since we'd come out. It had been a gold circle holding metal carved leaves painted gold, red and green. Now the wreath that decorated the door glimmered in silver and blue ribbons, glass balls, and tiny winking lights. A sprig of holly was stuck in the door knocker.

When we crested the steps of the porch, it started snowing. Flakes caught on our shoulders and in our hair.

"Someone will have to shovel the path in the morning," I commented.

"Not me," Ice said. "It's my least favorite job."

A smile pressed my lips. "Me, too!"

When we got inside and dusted off, an elf who was waxing the floor complained. "You're getting snow in here. Just move along, move along."

Ice actually chuckled.

I felt a laugh escape my own throat.

The elf glared at us. Before today, I might've done that glaring. Now I didn't care.

I shrugged off my coat and scarf, moving to the common room to hang them up.

Ice came up behind me and said, "You're limping."

"Just sore," I said. "I just pulled a muscle in my knee."

"You need a heating pad. You need to get off it."

Was he actually showing concern for me? I admit, I liked it.

"After we're done decorating. It barely hurts. I'm just favoring it."

"Suit yourself."

And there was that coldness again, so quick to possess him, like a storm churning inside that let up at its own rare whim.

Ice and I went to the storage room where we plundered boxes for wreaths and garlands.

"We don't want to over-do it." I shoved some boxes to the side.

"Why not?" Ice leaned down to open a box and his long hair fell forward in a bell-ringing wave.

"Because then things will just look like a mess again. Anyway, Jingle said not to."

Then Ice did something totally uncharacteristic. He bent at the waist and turned his hand palm up, extended out toward me. "I bow to your esthetic tastes."

I laughed. "Cut it out."

Suddenly he began to laugh with me. In the dust and the shadows, with boxes of glitter and glass orbs, we were having fun. Making the snowmen had been fun. When had things changed between us?

Or had they?

It was just a moment. I knew I should not make more of it. But I enjoyed laughing with him. In the snow. At the elf in the front room. And now.

Maybe Ice had some warmth burning deep within him. He just kept it well-hidden by his resentment, his irreverence. I still couldn't figure out why.

It took hours, but we managed to adorn each and every room of the workshop with just enough decorations to give the rooms a warm glow, a sweet glimmer. I had minimalist tastes. Ice liked the shinier trinkets. Together, our efforts collaborated into a quite pleasing outcome.

Jingle, looking a little ragged, his silver hair awash in his face, was amazed. He glanced at a few rooms to approve of what we'd done and said, "Well, you both have an eye for color and arrangement. Well done."

He did not speak directly to either of us, but Ice seemed to believe he was talking to me.

"Yes," Ice agreed. "Pepper is quite the artist."

Jingle turned to him and frowned good-naturedly. "I was speaking to both of you. You did this together, yes?"

We nodded.

"But Pepper's the real artist."

Jingle turned his head, as if already focused on another chore. "You both are. Take a break now. Get a few hours sleep."

It was already four in the morning. "Yes, sir," I said.

"Back here by nine sharp."

Ice was facing away from us now, as if unable to take even one, small compliment.

Jingle left the room, the accessories on his leather belt jangling. We were in the long-room again. A few elves were taking quick naps on some of the couches, but mostly it was empty.

Outside the dark sky made the ice cliffs look more ominous, though they were still beautiful, glitter-edged in starlight, casting gray and brown shadows on the frozen white fields below them.

The moon had begun to rise over the furthest ice precipice like a curved wedge of ivory. Or a piece of antler. Falling snow like tiny sapphires sparked the air where the lights from our now clean windows touched the flakes. Sometimes a sudden wind whipped them up into firefly swirls.

I leaned into one of the unoccupied couches, pillows at my back with the slight smell of camphor, and turned to put my feet up. My knee tried to protest. My grimace must have shown, because Ice said, "You need anything?"

"No, I think I'm going to just nap right here."

"All right." Surprisingly, he sat at the far end of my couch. He looked a little tired, so I figured he deserved to sit. But on my couch?

I didn't care. In fact, I liked his presence these last few hours. For all his surliness, it felt less lonely, in a way. I hadn't thought about being lonely in a long time. I was always surrounded by elves, work, the luxury of the workshop, and the esteem that accompanied working there.

It was strange how buoyant Ice's presence felt to me when he wasn't all that cheery himself. I had always liked his look, but that didn't mean his personality appealed. Yet, as I had been around him on this hectic day, I realized I'd made assumptions about him that had been in error. Even judgmental.

Now I was enjoying looking at him sitting at the end of the couch, resting his hand on the velvet arm. His rings flickered like caught starlight. Head up, his body leaned graceful as a swan into the cushions. His pale hair like drapes of silk. His long legs crossed at the knee.

I smiled to myself. My eyes ached from the long hours, but I didn't want to look away. I told myself I'd close them for a moment. One second only to regroup, re-arrange myself in the world.

Darkness swirled. Something soft and warm covered me. The fire crackled, mixing its soft burn into the air along with the sweet scents from the kitchen.

Something firm but soft brushed at my bangs, like the pads of fingers. I wanted to open my eyes but couldn't.

My lethargy could not be overcome. I sank deeper into the still nighttime of my mind, and the comfort of deserved rest.

Chapter Three

I stretched under cozy fleece, turning my head and opening my eyes.

The long-room basked in flaxen light. The fire in the hearth undulated. Snow still fell outside the windows. The sky was dark gray, edged with the possibility of sunlight along the cliff-side horizons.

I sat up. When had the blanket arrived? I tried to recall. Someone had draped it over me, but who? Ice?

My mind instantly declined the thought.

The end of the couch was vacant. Glancing about the room, I saw a few elves quietly napping, or drinking cocoa at the tables.

But Ice was nowhere in sight. I caught myself poised and listening for his ringing hair. Nothing.

Then I realized. Today was the day. I sat up straighter. Santa was coming!

A surge of anxiety rippled through my body. A mix of worry, excitement, and delightful anticipation.

I glanced at the room clock on the wall, a red circle with candy canes for hands. Eight o'clock. I had slept four hours. By nine, Santa would be here. I needed a shower. Fresh clothing. Maybe even a quick mug of cocoa. I needed to be at my best.

I folded the blanket, a square blue background dotted with snowflakes, and set it aside. When I stood, my knee gave a twinge, but only a little.

I noticed Pumpkin sitting alone, hands around his mug. He looked up when I approached.

"Hey, you're awake," he said.

"Did you get any sleep?" I asked.

"Not much. How about you?"

"Just a nap on the couch."

"How'd it go working with Ice?" asked Pumpkin.

"Fine." I looked about the room again. "He was here when I dozed off. Did you see him?"

"Nope. Did you guys hit it off? Is that why you're looking for him now?"

"Hit it off? What do you mean by that?"

Pumpkin just shook his head. "I told you he likes you."

"It's not like that." But I remembered now how much I'd enjoyed his presence for the past day. And his concern for me when I'd fallen and twisted my knee. The idea that as I'd fallen into a doze on the couch he'd been the one to cover me with a blanket made my skin heat. I thought of his pale eyes, his hair, his leanness. That surly tone that, now that I recalled it, made me smile.

"Pepper," he said. "You're so blind sometimes."

I shook my head, trying to clear my thoughts. "Well, anyway, what do you think of our decorating?"

He looked up at the garlands and ornaments, all arranged in tasteful increments about the room. "A blue-gold theme. Elegant."

"Thanks."

"Whose idea was it?"

"Mine, I guess."

"Well, you are the artist. Santa prizes your dolls almost above anything made here."

It was true. I had letters of commendation every year from Santa. Only about five percent of the elves in

27

Santa's Village received them. I had them framed and hanging on the walls of my cabin.

"Did you know," Pumpkin said, "that Ice has received none? Ever?"

"He's only been here a year."

"No, he worked here before you. Then he went away and came back."

"How old is he?" I asked.

Pumpkin shrugged. "How should I know? I never asked him."

"Wonder why he left?" I murmured my thought more to myself than to Pumpkin.

"For someone not interested in Ice at all, you sure ask a lot of questions about him."

"I do not."

He chuckled, batting his spoon at the melted marshmallows in his drink.

"Take it back." I pushed lightly on his broad shoulder.

Chimes rang behind me. I turned.

Ice stood in the long-room doorway watching us. I started to smile at him, but he made a rude gesture with his middle finger and vanished from sight.

"Hey...!"

Pumpkin turned to look. "What?"

"Ice was standing right there. He flipped me off."

Pumpkin looked under-whelmed. "Well, how long had he been there? Maybe he heard you say the decoration color-theme was all your doing."

"I did not say that!"

"You did. Blue-gold. All your idea."

"I—I—"

"Go after him if you want."

"I don't want. And you're wrong, Pumpkin. You're just wrong. We got a job done yesterday, and we did it well. That's it."

"Pepper, did anyone ever tell you you can be exasperating? And a little bit of a snob, too."

"What?"

Me? A snob? I was the one who'd just gotten flipped off.

"Yeah. You're pretty good at what you do. People admire it, but you just ignore them. You act as if it is your right and privilege that you're one of Santa's favorites. That you can make beautiful things as if it's no effort."

"But I put in long hours."

"Maybe that's the problem. You don't join in at the parties. You don't mingle so much, you know."

Tears came to my eyes. It felt as if Pumpkin was flipping me off right now, too. What had I done wrong? I blinked. My head was heavy from lack of a full night's sleep. My stomach felt sour. My eyes stung.

I swallowed hard. "I have to shower and change clothes before Santa comes."

Pumpkin, as if he didn't realize he'd hurt my feelings, quipped, "Hey. Coming to the party later tonight?"

Of course there would be a party. There always was after a visit from Santa. We elves could not keep our excitement to ourselves.

"Yeah, sure."

*

I trudged through the cold snow, head down, to my cabin. I didn't see anyone along the way, which was best. I was fighting grave disappointment in Pumpkin's implication that I acted snobby, and in Ice flipping me off, and didn't want it to infect anyone else's enthusiasm for the day.

I entered my cabin near the end of one of the village's snowflake arms. The shadowy interior greeted me with scents of piney candle-wax, the ashen burn of the hearth cold for a day and a night, old coffee. I took a deep breath, feeling my muscles instantly relax.

On my wall above my thick-pillowed couch hung my framed commendations from Santa. There was one for each of the five years I'd worked at the workshop. The gold frames lit up as I turned on a table lamp.

On the couch sat two of my earlier dolls, models that didn't quite make the cut for my first year, but which I had grown attached to. One had green hair, butterfly antennae, and a green silk dress. I called her Leaf. The other was more gothic, almost scary-looking, with a dark X over each eye for make up, his black hair shaved on the sides leaving a crest in the center of his scalp that stood up about three inches. He had a chain thick as my thumb around his neck, and dark narrowed eyebrows, but his lips were as pink and sweet as cotton candy. Outfitted in a tuxedo underneath the chain, he sat as if waiting for the end of the world instead of Christmas day. I had named him Fall.

I wanted to collapse on the couch and doze some more but I had no time for rest.

In the shower, surrounded by natural rock walls, I let the hot water patter against my skin. My knee was still slightly sore, but not stiff or swollen. Mostly, I could ignore the pain. I took my time standing in the fall of liquid heat after washing my hair and body.

Sometimes I had my most profound ideas for creativity while showering. With my mind relaxed, I would suddenly see images, designs I wanted to implement on my toys, color palettes, jewelry, facial expressions to paint.

But now, all I could think of was Ice, and over-riding that lovely image of the pale elf, Pumpkin's words slicing through me.

Pumpkin had thought nothing of his bluntness, as if he were telling me things I already knew. Or should know.

Eyes closed, letting the water wash away my aches, my fatigue, and maybe even a few tears, I realized that Pumpkin's misinterpretations of me were exactly what I'd been doing, mentally, to Ice. The difference was I'd never done it to his face.

But if Pumpkin was right, and Ice really did have a liking for me, could my past behaviors be seen by him as brush-offs when I really didn't mean it?

I wasn't a snob about my work. I told myself that over and over. It wasn't fair that Pumpkin had said that. I was simply modest. I didn't brag to others. I was even a little shy about my accomplishments. I wasn't one to go about drunk and crazy, pontificating about my exploits for all to hear. I wasn't that sort of person.

I asked myself if Ice had heard even part of my and Pumpkin's conversation. Did he think I took all the credit for the decorating?

But it could not be. We'd done everything together. We'd eventually made it fun for ourselves.

I vowed I would find Ice, explain things to him. But just the thought sent a shudder of fear through my body. And something else. Anticipation, maybe. Not unlike what I felt about Santa's visit. A surge of impending failure, as if I might lose something I did not yet have.

What a mixed up mess I was.

When I got out of the shower, I put on a soft white sweater, black trousers, and a black and white vest that nearly trailed the ground in tails behind me. It was a more formal look. For Santa.

I pinned a holly sprig at my top shirt button.

I carefully combed my hair back, gelling it a little so the feathers at the sides were more flat to accent my pointed ears, and made the few bangs on top sway artfully over my forehead.

I had been called handsome before. But all elves were. Everyone had a beauty about him or her in their own unique way. But I knew I looked good right now. If nothing else, I hoped Santa would be pleased.

I drew the shades up to let in a little of the dim, autumn light.

My bedroom had a four-poster, a stone hearth—unlit right now—and a colorful array of woven rugs. My nightstand held a lamp shaped like the crescent moon from early this morning. On its end hung a long-legged Santa made of glass, his joints wired together so that they moved. My tablet for reading lay below his feet.

As I stated before, we lived in luxury in Santa's Village. I loved my bedroom, my cabin, and working for Santa. And I held zero animosity toward others.

Yet Pumpkin had called me a snob.

I shook my head.

My stomach growled. But there was no time to eat. No time even for a mug of cocoa. I'd already taken too long in the shower.

Santa would arrive in fifteen minutes. It would take about five minutes for me to walk back to the workshop so I could check in with Jingle.

I needed to go.

Chapter Four

Harnesses of bells. Runners made of gold. Polished red sides. Seats of Corinthian leather.

Only four reindeer pulled the mighty sleigh, for Santa had a short drive along the main village road from his ice castle to the bustling workshop. No flying required.

The roadway glistened with new snow frozen to ice. A pine resin scent filled the air. The snorts of the deer and the patter of their feet were muted by the snowy silence. But the pilot's voice bellowed across the silvery air.

"Hohoho."

Santa had *arrived*!

He came beardless today, his look rustic, handsome, bronzed. He wasn't covered in soot. He didn't bring a bag of gifts. But he was wearing the red coat. It suited him with his wild gold hair that flew out behind him, his dark eyes and red lips.

Some said Santa was over a thousand years old. Jingle said he was not, but no one really knew. He never talked about his personal life in public. Almost everything anyone knew about him was based on rumors.

I had always heard he had never married. But that was only what I'd been told. Maybe there had been a Mrs. Claus once, and he simply never spoke of her. Or him.

Still, it was safe to say on our end of the village, no one really knew Santa. Not personally, anyway. He was friendly, generous, and our boss. That was it.

Probably it was the mystery of him that gave him more allure. We all revered and loved him.

As Santa exited his sleigh, two elves, Scamper and Snoball, rushed to meet him with a warm thermos of cocoa which they offered to him along with a ceramic chalice shaped like an angel whose wings were the handles. Two more elves approached the reindeer with treats, unbuckled them, and led them to our warm and cozy stable.

I did not know the reindeer by sight, but I heard others behind me mumbling, "That's Comet." "Look, he brought Dancer." "Isn't that Dasher2?"

I had only just arrived in time for Santa, and hadn't had a chance to look for Ice. Now I scanned the crowd as people started to file into the workshop. He was nowhere in sight.

My fists clenched. My body trembled as it always did when Santa was around. Nerves.

As Santa walked down the path, trailing the crowd, I heard him exclaim, "A snowman! A snow fairy! Exquisite work, my elves!"

I heard my name from the crowd. "Pepper. Pepper made them."

Santa sought my gaze and said across the snowy walkway. "Good work, Pepper!"

I grinned at him, nearly hopping up and down in my curl-toed shoes. "Ice helped, too."

"Oh, really?" He sent me a look of admonishment, as if he did not believe me.

"Yes. He made the wings on that one." I pointed at the fairy, hoping no one noticed the shaking in my hand.

Santa gave the fairy another glance, raised his bushy, golden eyebrows, and said nothing more about it.

My heart was beating fast. It was heady to see Santa. He only visited two or three times a year. Mostly, he sent notes. And commendations. But we all thrived because of him.

Once we were all inside, the kitchen elves served hot cocoa to everyone, and slices from a white cake sculptured like Santa's castle. Santa was so overcome with delight at the cake that his cheeks puffed out and turned red. He bounced up and down on the tips of his toes.

Jingle had made a rule we were not to bother Santa too abruptly on his arrival, letting him eat and drink in peace. His journey had not been a long one, but he was always famished, always wanting the treats we served.

I ate a few bites of cake, which Tinsel had perfectly baked, but it went down like a rock. I hadn't eaten since my toasted cheese sandwich late yesterday afternoon. My stomach was in knots.

I kept searching the room for Ice. What if he'd slept late? I was sure, even with his crass attitude, he wouldn't have wanted to miss this. I couldn't call him on the monitor. I had no clue where he lived, or his number.

Instead, I began to search for Syl. She might've been small, but she had a dramatic voice, a loud laugh. She was easy to find.

When I approached her, she lowered her brows at me. "Ah, is the lovely and talented Pepper gracing us with his presence?"

I looked behind her and saw North watching me.

Ignoring her almost-insult, I said, "Hi. Have you seen Ice? I've been looking—"

"He doesn't like these sorts of spectacles," she interrupted.

"What do you mean? He likes parties. He's always at them."

"Oh, so you noticed." She pouted. "You who didn't bother to attend the last three raves I threw."

I opened my mouth but no words came out. I wasn't sure how to respond. I hadn't meant to insult her, and I did like parties. Some parties. But in truth, I had more of a reclusive personality. I liked my books. I liked my hearth and home. I loved my job. What more could I want?

"I'm sorry I didn't come," I said. "I'm sure they were wonderful. In fact, I heard they were."

"Of course they were great. I'm fun. I throw fun parties after hours."

My mind spun as I stood there nodding at her. My thoughts scrambled. This was ridiculous. "So do you know where Ice is?"

She shrugged, her red dress going up and down stiffly. "Sometimes he hangs out in audio/visual on the third floor."

"Thanks."

Going up the stairs, my knee began to protest, but by the top of the landing it was all right. I walked without limping, my footsteps quiet, my freshly laundered clothes shushing softly.

Down two flights, I could hear the merriment. It sounded like Santa had finished his cake and wanted to begin the workshop tour.

The audio/visual room was located all the way at the end of the hall. When I opened the door, I saw Ice sitting at a computer, working on a game. I glimpsed dark figures flying across the screen. I had only seen brief shots of his newest game, but knew this had to be part of his baby project: *Vampire Crusade.*

"Is that the vampire thing?"

He looked up and shut off the device. "Maybe."

"Oh. Well, we were missing you downstairs."

He leaned back in the chair. "No you weren't."

"Did you get any sleep last night?" I noticed he still wore the same clothing he had on yesterday.

"Some."

Taking a risk, I decided to voice my suspicions of his secret kindness to me. "I know it was you who put the blanket over me in the long-room. Thank you."

He said nothing.

"Santa praised your snow fairy."

"It was your idea," he said.

"Not entirely."

"It was."

He seemed angry again. I did not understand.

"What's wrong with you?" I asked. I tried to keep my voice low. Unchallenging. "Santa loved the fairy. I told him you helped make it. He seemed impressed. What's the problem between you two?"

He spun a bit in his chair. His hair chimed. His fingers twinkled with rings.

"You really want to know?"

"Yes."

"He's pompous, arrogant, and nothing is good enough for him."

"I don't know why you'd say that. He's never said a bad word to any elf that I know."

"Yes, he's usually very polite." His face turned a little pink.

"Will you come downstairs with me and watch Santa tour the workshop?"

"Did Jingle send you to ask me?"

"No."

It was true, though, that Jingle had required every elf to be in attendance this morning. Ice risked his job by being contrary.

"Then why are you here?" Ice asked. "You don't even like me."

"I'm sorry you think that about me, but it's not true."

"It is."

"No, it isn't. I thought you hated me. Whenever I saw you, it seemed like you were always glaring at me."

"I don't glare."

I laughed.

"All right. Maybe I do. But you're so standoffish, Pepper. As if no one's good enough for you. You're like Santa that way. So annoying."

"I feel like you know Santa more than the rest of us. How is that?"

He put a hand to his forehead and rubbed. "Somewhat, yes, I do."

"Well, are you ever going to tell me why?"

"Probably not."

I sighed. "Come on. Just come back downstairs with me. I don't want you in trouble with Jingle."

To my surprise, he rose from the chair, graceful and alluring, despite not having much rest, a shower, or a change of clothing. The air practically sparkled around him. The knots in my stomach untied, then tied themselves up again tighter. I wanted to smile at his beauty. I wanted to cry out.

Instead, I said softly, "There's cake."

He let out a long breath. "Well, damn, I like cake."

What elf didn't?

Ice followed me down two flights of stairs. My knee took them gingerly, but I managed.

*

Santa took his time on the tour, stopping in every specialty room of the workshop, admiring everything, giving praise. We elves loved to puff and preen from praise. We took pride in our work.

His third stop was my shop. He exclaimed over my dolls. They were always among his favorites. They may have been old-fashioned compared to the videos and games Ice and Syl and North were involved with, but they were a hit because of that.

"One-of-a-kind art," Santa said about them. "They shine."

I noticed that when Santa spoke to me, he looked just to my side. Ice was there, standing very still, and Santa seemed more intent on him than me. It was killing me that I didn't know what was between them.

I could not believe they'd been lovers once. Ice seemed too young. But then again, I had no idea how old he really was. We elves age very slowly.

The very air around Ice snapped with tension. I felt it all along my back and sides. And Santa, when his gaze went to Ice, changed in demeanor as well. His face darkened. His jolly-ness dissipated, though no one else appeared to notice.

Santa lingered over my work-station, which only made matters worse. For he kept praising me. And I felt Ice grow tenser with each moment.

"I'm not surprised," Santa said, "that you were the elf responsible for the ice fairy as well."

"Well, Ice did most of that one," I said.

"But I know you were the influence," Santa countered.

My heart stopped for a second. I couldn't believe he'd said that. My face heated. Mortified, I had the urge to reach a hand out to Ice and grip it.

"No," I said, trying to keep my voice from shaking. "It was his idea to do something non-traditional."

"Yes, he is non-traditional at his best," Santa said. And it wasn't a compliment.

I heard Ice whisper under his breath, "Fucking hell."

Some whispering started in the crowd. The elves nearest me looked worried, but they brightened up quickly when Santa announced he was moving on.

I realized only then I'd been holding my breath.

I turned to Ice. He tried not to meet my gaze, but I was persistent. "What in all the worlds--?"

Ice's hair pinged as he shook his head hard. "He's incapable of seeing the real me." Then he looked directly at me. "Just as you were, Pepper."

"I didn't—I don't." I was stuttering.

A slow smile that depicted anything but joy curved his lips. "You're a traditionalist, too."

Hotly, "I am not!"

"Dolls, Pepper. Dolls."

His words sounded like insults.

"What's wrong with dolls?"

Besides, Santa had just gone out of his way to praise them.

"I'm just saying," Ice muttered. "There's traditional. And then there's the rest."

My eyes stung. I liked Ice. Truly. At least now I did. I'd even defended him. But if our values were so different, were we fated to only fight? To rasp against each other like sandpaper?

Then I remembered the ice fairy. She was stunning, elegant, our harbinger of the season. A Pepper and Ice collaboration. We had won with her. Both of us. Praise and admiration. We'd made something out of nothing with only a bit of snow and two spoons.

"You said I hated you," I said. "But you must truly despise me. You have nothing but ire for what I do."

"Oh fuck, first Santa, now you."

"But you didn't let me finish. There's the fairy. That was awesome."

"Yet everyone thinks it's all you."

"They don't."

He made a snort of disgust, and headed out of the room ahead of me, following the crowd down the shining, golden hall.

Two stops later, we were in electronics. I thought maybe Ice would dodge it by spiriting himself away to the third floor again. Instead, he stood centermost in the room. He wouldn't look at me. Syl and North explained some of the newest inventions and games.

Santa loved it all, of course. Jingle stood by, arms crossed, looking proud as if we were all his wunderkinds.

Syl said, with a flourish of her hand and a flair to her voice, "Our newest and favorite new game for the season is *Vampire Crusade.* Just look at that art, and the movement. And of course I play half the characters, and North does the rest. Ice wrote the entire storyline and programmed it. Took him months including over-time. It's modern and addictive, just what the kids are wanting these days."

"Vampires for Christmas?" Santa questioned.

Syl's eyebrows rose higher, trying to sell it. "Why, yes. The action. The excitement. It's all the rage. And the storyline gets deeply metaphysical. You should see this clip." She reached out to turn on a giant, wall-sized monitor.

Santa held his hand up. "Ice wrote that storyline, yes?"

Syl nodded mutely.

"I don't need to see it."

"Of course you don't." Ice's tone came out bland. Bored. "You never do."

My heart beat in my throat as I watched Ice blithely mouth off. He could be rude. Most of us could when provoked. But not to Santa, *never* to Santa.

The whole room was silent. As if all the elves forgot how to breathe.

Ice continued, as if no one else could hear. As if the merriment of our crowd had never been real. "You are stuck in time. You know this. And it's insulting to the rest of us who can never be good enough for you, those of us who don't paint beguiling doll-faces, who do think outside the box, and have grand ideas—"

Santa held his hand up. "Ho!" His voice was not cruel, but it was loud. "Enough!" His face grew dark, his green eyes fierce. He had firm control over the whole room with that tone, with his large presence, with his amazing charisma. But Ice was unaffected.

"You shut me up, put me down. Every time. You don't believe I can make anything beautiful."

A collective gasp rose up from every elf in the room.

"Of course I do." Now Santa's tone came out more soothing. "But vampires for Christmas? All here would agree with me it is inappropriate. Wouldn't you?" He turned to face the room.

Elves nodded vigorously, trying to do good, to be on the right side.

Then Santa turned his gaze on me. "Pepper, you have an aesthetic eye. What do you think?"

It was as if all the breath had been pushed from my lungs. I had never really seen Ice's vampire game, only some beautiful production shots. I had no clue what to say. The room was too hot. My heart pounded.

Santa was looking to me. It was a moment of power. And great discomfort. Santa was our leader, the greatest elf ever. But behind me I could feel Ice in a strange, tall serenity, like a magnificent frozen sculpture refusing to be melted by the sun.

Whatever was happening, it was between Ice and Santa. Being caught in the middle was pure torture.

"Well, what do you think?" Santa prodded.

"I honestly cannot say. I have not played the game. But the production shots I saw are vivid and inspired." I thought that was a fair statement. Always, I wanted to take Santa's side. I'd built him up in my mind to be almost a myth. He couldn't be wrong. And I thrived on his approval. But Ice deserved more than this.

"But," Santa said with a smile, holding his hand up as if he had hypnotized the crowd. "You can see my thinking on this, that vampires are not an appropriate Christmas theme."

I gulped. "You asked for my aesthetic eye, sir."

Santa sighed. "Yes. I did." The strong voice carried through me with a powerful sense of disappointment.

"I can say, then, that the beauty of the art, the form, the characters—all of it is quite appealing—"

Santa held up his hand, interrupting. "That will be all, then, on this matter. The project is cancelled."

This couldn't be happening. Santa's disapproval felt like a hard slap, and I had not done anything wrong.

A fever fueled the air around me. The light from outside turned white, a single glare off a fissure in a cliff piercing my eyes. Dust motes swam before me, as if in an intelligently choreography ballet.

I had to make things right.

"But—but Santa, of course you are, in general, right. But it does seem as if you are maybe rushing—"

It was too late. My voice too small, too soft. Santa had already turned away from me, smiling at the rest of the elves, spreading his arms to include them in his aura. Ice had heard me, though. I heard him hiss, "Kiss up, that's what you do best."

I huffed. My breath hitched. How could he say that? I had defended his project.

I realized I was shaking. My knee began to ache. Sweat rolled down my back under my clean white shirt. I turned to see Ice, bare arms crossed over his chest, muscles tight, staring at me. But it wasn't the stare that got to me, it was those blue eyes, as still and deep as I'd ever seen them, glistening with hurt. He projected that hurt onto me, as if I had been the one to cancel his project.

"Ice—" I began.

He turned away and shifted into the crowd, his back to me, the bells of his hair echoing to a grave distance in my mind.

I took a few shallow breaths, trying to compose myself. An arm came around my shoulder from behind. I whirled.

"Well," said Pumpkin jovially. "That could have gone a little better. Why didn't you tell him what he wanted to hear?"

"Who? Santa?"

"Who else do you think I meant?" he said with a sly grin.

I lowered my eyes. The floor looked like a liquid wave, but Pumpkin's arm steadied me.

"It's not the end of the world," Pumpkin said.

"I—I didn't know what to say." The words came out in one whoosh of breath.

Pumpkin squeezed my shoulder. "Of course you knew what to say. You just hesitated because your own opinion wasn't what Santa wanted to hear. But you stood your ground. 'Bout time you grew some balls."

"But I ended up failing to get my opinion across anyway."

Pumpkin's breath spiced my cheek. "It's okay. No big deal. Nothing will be worse for you."

He steered me into the hall, but I was no longer interested in joining the crowd for the rest of the tour. Jingle might've required the presence of us all, but in that moment I didn't care.

I ducked away from Pumpkin's hand on my shoulder.

He looked at me in question.

I made a quick excuse. "I'm just going to get another piece of cake."

Pumpkin sighed. "Santa still loves you best."

But Santa wasn't the only elf I'd somehow disappointed.

Downstairs, a couple of kitchen elves were gathering dirty plates and cups into bins and carting them to the washer. I didn't recall their names.

"Hurry," said one. "I want to get upstairs in time to see the rest of Santa's tour."

"I'm going as fast as I can," said the second.

Neither of them paid attention to me as I approached the once beautiful cake and stared at the wreck of Santa's miniature castle. The elves disappeared into the kitchen.

My hands were still shaking. I could not get rid of the heavy feeling in my chest. Cake was the last thing I wanted.

I went to the front window. Ice glistened along the elf-tracks on the pathway and in the sleigh runnels on the road. The sky was shadowy, clouding the weak daylight. The frost fairy and snowman gazed at one another across the soft, white ground. I had the strangest feeling of sadness when I looked at the fairy, yet the memory of constructing her was one of utmost pleasure. Snowdrops had started to fall on us as we created her. As Ice finished shaping the last fret of her wings, he had looked at me through the white flakes and smiled. Not a big smile. Just a mild up-curve at the sides of his mouth.

Heat moved through me at the memory of that small response. His almost-smile. His relaxed stance of modesty at his own pleasure in his accomplishment.

I blinked and the scene blurred, my own reflection ghosting the window. I realized even though I'd complimented Ice's game, I had not taken enough of a stand for Ice in the presence of Santa. I had failed him. And now there I was in the window's mirror, transparent and unreal, feeling misunderstood, feeling as if I should apologize for everything I'd said and done in the past day.

My skin burned hot underneath my clothing. Embarrassment. Or so I told myself. But accompanying that was a strange longing for Ice. A yearning for his approval and attention. A strange attraction.

Of course I could not blame him for hating me before we had been assigned to work together, and now afterward.

Yet hate had not sculpted an elaborate fairy in a snow garden. Hate had not covered me with a warm blanket as I fell into exhausted sleep. Hate had not sent me a private half-smile under a northern, dusky, October sky.

Hard-won gestures, all. And I felt I had betrayed them. Betrayed him.

I raised my hands to my face and pressed.

This would not do! Jingle might have occasionally called me "dark and broody", but in reality I was a fairly happy elf. If anyone was broody, it was Ice.

I told myself I didn't need someone so complicated in my life. I'd been fine before Ice. I'd be fine afterward. What I needed more than anything was quietude, maybe a real meal, and some sleep.

I heard the pattering on the upper stairs of Santa and dozens of elves moving to the third floor. I should have been among them. Instead, I could not stand to be in the workshop for one more minute.

My cabin wasn't far. I simply opened the workshop's front door and headed for the icy road.

The outside temperature had dropped quite abruptly since Santa had arrived. I was so hot and aggravated, though, I did not notice it at first. The cold had created a frozen glaze over everything.

But I was used to snow and ice. My feet knew automatically how to pick their way to the areas that were rougher or made of more gravelly ice. But the slipperiness was bad. So I veered toward the deeper snow off the road, letting my legs slog through the knee-deep drifts.

The snow fell faster now, flakes spiraling and swooping as a cold breeze swept through the village. Suddenly, a wind came up from the direction of the great glacier at the edge of the Village furthest from Santa's castle. It hit me like a dozen knives.

I gasped. All the sweat from my body froze. The air whitened with more snow, and I couldn't help but breathe it in, the sting of it on my lips and tongue.

This instant blast could mean only one thing. I looked up. The sky was black.

Blizzard.

How stupid of me not to have seen it as soon as I'd come outside. Though it was unexpected, and no weather warning had come, I'd lived in the North Pole long enough to know that these sorts of storms could gather fast out of nowhere.

I could still see the line of cabins I was headed for, and mine was only third down the row. I knew I could make it to my doorstep, but now the road was yards away and I was pushing through freezing drifts of snow. It hampered my progress.

If the road weren't so slippery, I could easily have jogged to my cabin in a couple of minutes.

Now all my muscles became sluggish. My body was one big ache. My jaw shuddered so hard my teeth knocked together. I gritted them and pushed forward as hard as I could, cutting through the snow with my now numb feet, forcing myself to keep moving.

A fierce, stabbing pain went through my knee, tripping me. I caught my balance and kept going.

I had no head covering, no parka, no mittens, no scarf. How could I have been so negligent?

The wind grew crueler, as if it had long arms and thick fists, pummeling me right and left. I fell several times, my bare hands burning from the freeze as I caught myself on them deep in the thick snowdrifts.

It seemed like I'd been pushing myself forward forever, yet I had not yet reached the first cabin. But the snow was blowing so thick now, I couldn't see. Maybe I'd passed it. Maybe I'd turned without even knowing and was headed behind the cabins and toward the distant tundra.

I couldn't feel my hands anymore. My face felt like it was splitting in half. The cold stung and bit until I could barely feel it.

Then a sweet warmth washed over me. One more step, I thought. Just one more. But I couldn't move my back foot forward. My injured knee had locked and wouldn't cooperate. The wind tossed itself over me and through my clothing, under my vest and shirt, into my eyes and ears. Shoving. Shoving.

I felt myself fall—

The wind called my name in a voice of wolves and hunger. Then it softened, and within its angry howls, I heard it say, "You stupid, stupid elf."

It definitely had hands, for it was pushing me again. Tugging. I cried out, but it stole my voice as soon as it left my throat.

Something white—a fall of snow?—drifted over me. Encompassed me. Buried me.

Then I felt something under my arms. And a dizzying weightlessness.

That meant loss of consciousness was only seconds away.

I was dying.

Chapter Five

White on white. My world, my spirit, my soul became encased in a tiny, insignificant crystal.

I was nothing, and nothing had come to claim me.

The wind kept talking. Lifting. Calling me names. "Idiot." "Moron." "Buffoon." And worse.

I wanted to tell it: "My name is Pepper." But it had thieved my voice along with my soul.

Like a weird echo, it repeated a phrase I'd heard moments—or maybe hours ago. "You stupid, stupid elf."

A kindling warmth, still too cold to recognize, pressed my stomach and chest. I kept passing in and out of consciousness, opening my eyes to white again and again. But the whiteness was solid now, quilted. It looked more like cloud than snow.

I heard my own voice moaning, crying. I tried to move. That was when I realized I was being carried. My limp arms flopped forward against someone's back. My legs dangled against someone's chest and waist.

"Hush, I've got you."

Everything that was white went dark.

*

When I opened my eyes, I saw a thin orange light in surrounding darkness. A heaviness covered me, but not cold or wind anymore. It was solid, soft, yielding. And the roar of the wind had subsided to a distant rage, its anger seeking other prey.

"Good thing you have dark hair and clothing. If you were my coloring, you would have blended in so well I might not have found you."

Haloed by the wavering orange-ness, Ice stood looking down at me. One silver bell caught in a wind-tangled braid winked at me.

"I—I--" I couldn't yet speak. My throat felt raw. When I tried to move I realized my body was still so cold that my joints were locked.

Ice moved closer to me with a grace and poise I envied. He still had snow in his braids and loose locks, and in the folds of his knitted cap. He did not look warm at all, but he definitely was not frozen like me.

He moved closer, closer. I wasn't sure why until I realized he was shoving his arm behind me, helping me to sit. With his free hand he held a mug near my face and its steam met my skin like a caress.

The drink smelled like peppermint tea.

"Try to take a sip," he said.

I barely felt the edge of the mug against my lips. The hot liquid scorched its way down my throat. Singed sugar. Burning mint. Only a sip, but it seared me to the bottom of my stomach. I coughed, leaning hard against Ice's supporting arm.

Slowly, my eyes adjusted to the darkness and I could see the room about me. Not my cabin, but similar. The walls were made of darker rock than mine. The wood ceiling was a natural gold, while mine was painted white.

A soft springy-ness supported me. A couch.

Pillows and a tossed white parka lay strewn on the floor. Soft white rugs flowed up to a low table, two recliners and a desk.

Ice had changed his clothes since I last saw him. He wore silver leggings and a silver tunic beneath an open white sweater. He wore a white knit cap, but his hair was loose. The silver bells may have made sounds but I did not hear them, their delicacy lost to the pounding of my own heart and my still-loud rasping breaths.

He forced me to take another sip of the tea. This time I did not cough, and bent my head for more. It warmed me inside, but my legs and hands still tingled with cold. I couldn't feel my toes.

Ice's hand came up, rings flashing, and pushed the hair back from my forehead. It came away wet and I felt water trickle down my temples and jaw.

"I saw you leave," he said quietly. His pale eyes shifted over my face, peering at me as if I were some mysterious anomaly. "What were you thinking?"

I tried to move my hand to take the mug, but realized it was held fast by the heaviness over my body which consisted of thick blankets.

But all the blankets were doing was keeping the cold in. I needed to move closer to the hearth.

I lowered my eyes as my whole body began to violently shudder under the blankets. I gasped in answer. "I just wanted to go home."

He shook his head, the tea in the mug sloshing a bit. "Stupid."

"Stop calling me that." My eyes warmed and overflowed as if melting. I turned my head, my body shuddering, struggling against the blankets.

"You went without even a coat."

I ignored his comment, shoved at the heavy blankets and got my arms free. I swiped at my face, rubbing.

Ice grabbed my wrists in his hands. "Don't. You'll chafe the skin."

"I need to get closer to the fire." Every word was hard to get out. My chest shook. My lungs quivered.

"Can you move?"

I pushed with my legs. My knee screamed in pain, but I managed to sit all the way up.

Without a word, Ice put his arm under mine and around my upper back, helping me up. I stumbled, leaning heavily against him. He was so warm I wanted to wrap my body around his and just go limp. Instead, I collapsed on some pillows by the fire.

He draped my shoulders with a blanket and handed me my tea.

I almost couldn't hold the mug, but already the fire was thrashing its heat into my skin. I used both hands to keep the mug upright. Its heat bled into my palms, fingers, wrists. The sensation curled like a promise of ecstasy up my arms. The fire's heat had already worked into my feet and legs. My back still felt cold, even with the blanket. My knee throbbed, but things were rapidly improving.

Ice sat close by my side, reaching for his own mug of tea which was sitting on the hearth. His presence warmed me even more than the fire. My veins tingled, sleet turning to warm, red rain. Dots of heat sparked in my stomach and chest.

We sipped together in silence, the minty sweetness of the drink like paradise in the north. Especially after almost dying.

Finally, Ice broke the silence. "I saw you leave. I thought you'd be right back since you'd forgotten your coat and scarf."

"I wasn't thinking."

"Understatement of the year."

I glanced at him, frowning.

He frowned back. "Seriously, Pepper, you can't be that sensitive over Santa."

I blinked, my eyes warming. My breath caught. My pulse revved. His nearness was so warm. I wanted to lean into him again. My body tensed pleasantly at the thought.

More snow melted from my hair and trickled icily down the back of my neck.

I pulled the blanket tighter and stared into the blue-gold flames.

"It wasn't just Santa," I said.

He kept staring at me until I looked away.

"It was everything." I took a deep, shaky breath. "It's my fault your project was cancelled. I'm so sorry. I should have spoken up louder for you."

Ice rolled his eyes. "Santa was going to cancel it anyway."

"No he wasn't. You were right to call me a kiss up."

"I shouldn't have said that. I was pissed at the moment."

"I know. I deserved it."

"I wasn't really pissed at you, Pepper. What you said about my game was nice." His tone went quiet. "Not everything revolves around you, you know. I was angry with Santa."

That confused me. It always had. Every elf I knew loved Santa. We would not be working in the Village if we didn't like it.

"But why?" I asked.

He turned away, closing himself off again.

"Don't do that," I said.

"Do what?"

"Shut down like that."

"I'm not." But he did not look up.

"I know you're not fond of me, but—"

His hand came up, palm out. "Stop. You make so many quick assumptions."

"Am I wrong?"

"Yes! Dammit, Pepper, I don't hate you. You're just such a favorite of Santa's. And I happen to have a reaction to Santa's pets."

"What? That make's no sense." I didn't brag about Santa's favoritism, or my commendations. But I had been accused of being a snob in the past 24 hours. And honestly, I enjoyed all praise from Santa. And my Santa-commendations were framed and hung on a prominent living room wall in my cabin. Was he merely jealous?

I said, "I take pride in my work, but I don't mean for it to come across that I'm superior."

He glanced sidelong at me, his eyebrows raised.

"I mean, you take pride in what you do. That *Vampire Crusade* game. I can tell you're proud of it."

He lowered his chin slightly as if in agreement.

And that's when I saw the problem with more clarity. It wasn't about pride. It was about values. Our conflicting values about appeasing the boss brought an unconscious friction between us. Ice was known for his snide comments about Santa, and an almost arrogant disrespect. I was known for praising everything Santa-related, and chasing the internal pride that came with pleasing the old elf. I was the follower, Ice the skeptic.

It was probably the biggest reason why our paths had not crossed until now. People tended to avoid those they thought they had nothing in common with.

But in the last day we had learned we worked well together. We could get along. In fact, there was an attraction that could not be denied. Pumpkin's assurance that Ice "liked" me made my stomach do funny flips.

We had differing value systems about our placement in our jobs and how our lives were affected by it. But so what? Was that such a big deal?

We both sat and stared at the fire. I wondered if similar thoughts were going through Ice's mind.

His shoulders hunched. A surge of empathy spread through me, a little flame edging the center of my heart.

"Tell me this, then," I said after awhile. "How did you see me leave anyway? And when did you change your clothes?"

"I left the electronics room before you did and decided to go downstairs to the locker room. I had a change of clothes there. But I didn't care about that. Really, I was avoiding the crowd. It just all seemed so silly after he—after his comments about inappropriateness. He's clueless about the 21st century. I was in the hall when you came down, and I thought maybe Santa had cut the tour short. But you were alone."

My gaze lingered on the damp ends of his hair, how they curled as they started to dry. His silver tunic caught the light in imperfect reflections of dark bronze and pale yellows.

He continued, "You were so still. Maybe a bit upset. I was about to speak to you when you rushed out the door with no coat, nothing."

"Oh," I replied. He'd seen me. He'd also read my emotional state correctly. I *had* been very upset. Still was.

"Why did you leave like that?"

Shame washed my cheeks. "I just wanted to go home. It's not that far and I wasn't thinking. I didn't see that the temperature had dropped, or notice the blizzard coming. I didn't even feel it until I'd gone too far to turn back."

"Yes," he said with a sigh. "I know that. Your behavior was a bit disconnected. It concerned me."

"Concerned you?"

"Of course."

I looked into his sea-blue eyes, then back down at my lap where my hands were folded together, still slightly shaking.

I heard a shift of cloth, an errant bell trapped in a blond braid as he moved closer. He said, "How's your knee?"

The question, a simple, rational query, was suddenly the loveliest thing I'd ever heard. Because Ice was asking. Because he remembered that moment in the snow when I'd fallen while we'd been building the snowman.

"It hurts."

"Take off your pants."

"What?" My head came up. I searched his face for animosity, disgust, or teasing humor. I found none.

Instead, he held up another blanket, a soft afghan made of yarn from Russian sheep. "You can put this over your lap," he suggested. "I just want to see if it's swollen."

"Yeah. Okay." My hands slipped over the fastenings, still ice cold. I lifted my hips and pulled down the black trousers, so formal for Santa.

Beneath them, I wore lime green underwear edged in soft white fur. It's an elf-thing. Plus, they were my favorites, so soft and comfortable against the skin.

I saw Ice's eyes glance down. I grabbed the blanket from him and pulled it to my waist.

With no inhibition, he pushed the afghan away from my leg and exposed my knee. It didn't look too bad, but there was some swelling around the knee-cap. His hands gently cupped it on either side, pale against my coppery skin.

"Does that hurt when I touch it?"

His bare skin against mine was electric.

"No." I shook my head, trying not to show how much his touch was affecting my body. "If I bend it, then it hurts a little."

His hands were warm, gentle.

"You're too cold for an ice pack. A heating pad, maybe?"

"No, it's all right," I said.

As if he did not hear me, he got up and went to another part of the house.

I made myself more comfortable in my nest of blankets and tried to relax. My hands were still cold and I held them closer to the fire.

I found a plush pillow and put it behind me, lying back, my feet toward the fire. I must've dozed off, because I jerked when I heard a sound by my left side. My eyes opened from a rapid dream. I remembered only that I'd been basking in an ocean of swirling blues and greens.

Ice had returned. He knelt beside me, setting a tray laden with bowls on the rug. He had a heating pad under his arm and pushed the blanket back from my leg again, spreading the pad over my knee and plugging in the cord to an outlet beside the hearth.

Outside, I could hear the wind desperately searching as if it had lost a part of itself in the cold and the white.

Inside, in Ice's cabin, the fire burned merrily.

"I figured it's been awhile since you ate." He gestured toward the tray as I straightened to a sitting position.

I could not hold back my smile. I'd already smelled the chicken soup. But beside two bowls sat two rather lumpy and blackened toasted cheese sandwiches.

"I'm not as good as you at making the sandwich, as you can see."

I wanted to laugh. "They're better burnt anyway."

He scowled.

"Seriously," I said. "The blackened crust mixed with the cheese is great. Try it. Yum."

Ice picked up a sticky, misshapen sandwich and brought it to his lips. His teeth bit into it, white and straight. I watched him chew and swallow.

"You're right," he said, then took another bite.

"Thank you," I said. "You didn't have to do all this."

"Of course I didn't have to," he agreed.

I reached for my sandwich. It was hot against my still-cold finger tips. I took a bite and it tasted so good I finished in about three, big bites.

"Hmm," said Ice. "You were hungry." He handed me a bowl of soup.

Together we ate and listened to the wind.

The best part of this day, which had started off so poorly, was him sitting next to me. Yes, he had rescued me, and that was wonderful. But the little things, like the soup, and the way the firelight danced upon his tunic, and in his hair, those were so good. I thought I might never grow tired of his presence which exuded a faint scent of vanilla cream, and even his surliness,

56

when I looked back on it, was part of his hot/cold allure.

It didn't feel strange when he finally set the tray aside, all the dishes empty, and said, "You are welcome to stay as long as you like. And rest."

"Well, I can't really leave. Don't you hear that wind?" It gusted. It cried. It heaved itself against rooftops and walls.

He nodded. "It's wild. But I pulled up the forecast on my monitor. The blizzard will pass by in the early morning hours." He blinked and quickly looked away, almost as if shy.

I knew what he was offering. That I could stay. That if I wanted to, I could spend the night.

"Ice," I said, stretching my legs out, the heat on my knee loosening it up.

He raised his eyebrows. "What?"

"Show me *Vampire Crusade*."

"Really?"

"Yes. I'd really love to try it out."

His face opened. His eyes twinkled. He jumped up. "Okay!"

His coffee table hid a large monitor that rose from the center when he pushed a panel button.

Soon, we were back on the couch, me in my green underwear and white shirt and vest, with plenty of blankets to warm me, and Ice with his legs curled under him, a fluffy red pillow in his lap.

The game was brilliant, a work of art. Vampires under dazzling sunsets, or hanging off crescent moons, haunted every corner of this game. There were good ones and bad ones. And the war was on.

He'd spared no detail. The violence was gruesome. The characters were more sad and funny than scary, and prone to fall in love. You had no clock to beat. Instead, it was all in the timing of the sun. It rose and fell in purple increments, and if you made mistakes and lost ground, the sun came back faster, the true vampire's enemy.

We spent the whole afternoon playing, Ice showing me his world.

He turned to me and said, "What do you think?"

"I love it."

He set his control down and reached for my hand. "Thank you for saying that."

His fingers pressed the back of my wrist.

I turned my hand over and gripped his, palm to palm.

The day, with its beginnings in hell. Now it only kept getting better.

Chapter Six

It had happened quickly, these feelings inside me, and yet they'd been gradually building since yesterday. This attraction for Ice. Now he held my hand, and it made everything real and immediate. My skin flared with warmth.

Though I wanted him with all my heart, right then and there, he did not make a move to kiss me. Perhaps he was waiting for me to do it. Or he still had questions about his feelings. Or maybe he was just shy. Though I could not quite match that description to his often-indignant personality.

He stood gracefully, like a pale golden deer under deep, gold moonlight, and held out his hand. "Come with me."

I reached up. He pulled me from the couch to my feet, careful to see that I did not wrench my knee. I wrapped the biggest blanket about my shoulders and body, and followed him across the living room.

I had been warm for a long time. Even my bare feet were warm now, and my icy socks and shoes had been set aside by the fire to dry.

I wondered if Santa had gone back to his castle by now. He had more power than any regular elf, and could fly in all weather. Somehow, his mind was able to create electromagnetic fields and pathways that blocked outside stimulus so he could navigate fog, blizzards and rainstorms. Most elves were not born with such powers. That was why Santa was Santa Claus.

Ice led me to the kitchen were he had spiked cider already heated in a glorified coffee maker. He poured us each a full mug. He tipped his up to his parted lips. I blew on mine and sipped. It was sweet and burning at the same time.

"Ready for a tour of the rest of my place?" he asked.

I took another sip of the hot drink, swallowing hard. "I am."

I didn't care that his cabin was the exact same floor plan as mine. I wanted to see it. This was Ice's home. And I had been invited in.

We took our mugs down a short hall, all wood beams, the ceiling and wall flickering from light leaking in from the living room. There were two back rooms, a study which I could tell he never used, containing only a desk piled high with electronics, and a single desk chair. The curtains against the window were dark maroon. The floor was bare of rugs.

The second room, the master bedroom, stretched the length of the back of the cabin, just like mine, with two windows shrouded in white, and a connected bath.

When he turned on the lights, there was no one source of illumination. Small lamps and lanterns were scattered about but controlled by one switch. A line of white lights made a downward curve on the wall above his headboard.

The room smelled a little of pine, and the cleanliness of air right after a rain. A hearth, unlit, took up space near the door.

Two dressers, a bedside table, and throw rugs in hues of purple and green made the room homey, but were accents only for the real centerpiece. The bed. It was unmade. Obviously, he had not expected to bring anyone here, or he didn't care about such amenities as fluffed pillows and unwrinkled bedspreads.

I know I didn't care. I saw thin, shallow folds in the sheets and longed to touch them, knowing they'd be soft from the weight of his body and sweet with his scent. Maybe it was the room, or maybe the cider, but I immediately felt comforted by my surroundings. No tension here. Just peace. Which seemed almost incongruous for all Ice's complaining, and yet not. Here was where he could be himself without prying eyes, judgment, or fear. We all had need of safe places in our lives, whether it was with friends who connected with us, or in our work, or at home in shaded bedrooms of our own making.

I had no words to describe my contentment that didn't sound shallow or ridiculous. Instead, I smiled, made myself at home and sat on the foot of his bed, wrapping my blanket tighter about my shoulders.

He stood very still and looked at me, one arm tight against his sternum, the other hanging limp at his side. His face held no expression, no judgment, but not quite the assuredness one might hope to see on the face of a potential lover. Then he moved to the window, pulled back the curtain and looked out at the cold blaze of storm.

Here in the back of the cabin, though it might seem exposed to the wilderness beyond the village, the sound of the storm was less. It was because drifts of snow tended to pile up toward the back line of all the cabins and mute the outside world.

I wondered what time it was. Then didn't I care as I took in more of the room.

I loved his lamps, little golden globes set here and there, and one with reddish tones on his nightstand where an empty glass stood next to a stack of books and notebooks, a tablet, and a pile of silver rings.

Ice let the curtain to the window fall and turned to face me. "Do you need anything?"

I shook my head. I did not need. I wanted. And because his hearth was bare, I longed to get under the covers of his bed to escape the thin chill. But I did not move.

He came over to the foot of the bed and sat beside me. His hair jingled. I took a deep breath of his clean scent.

For a second—and only a second—I worried that he was sitting there not as a prelude to touching me, but as a friendly gesture to let me down easy. But the way his face looked in the lamplight, his pale eyes glistening as they gazed up and down my blanketed form, banished that worry at once.

Again, he held one long arm crossed against his body just above his waist. His other hand, palm down on the spread, held the weight of his torso as it slightly leaned.

Slowly, I reached out from the folds of my blanket and put my hand over his on the bed. I saw his lips part, but barely. His head tilted back, and the shadows on the walls turned soft.

He moved back on the bed, and my fingers curled about his hand, holding on. He tugged me back with him and I knew. The day was turning. No. Not just the day. My life. Taking a left on a new path.

I could already feel the muted velvet of the air enfolding me. The absolute purity of finding something you did not know you had ever lost. My heartbeat tangled with desire: wordless, instinctive. It was that incredible moment of utter beauty mixed with trepidation, because this was not at all casual for me.

A feeling grew from the pit of my stomach up to my chest, an energy you could not see or hear, but that was more powerful, even, than the outside storm.

I lay on the tousled covers on my side, my blanket falling back and revealing my shirt, my green briefs, my bare legs. Our clasped hands rested between us.

I was afraid to make the first move. Our eyes locked. He did not look away. I watched the way his dark pupils began to expand against the glowing aquamarine of his irises. Beyond the physical, a connection was being made here by just looking at each other. Just seeing. It was as if we needed that extended moment to slowly lower the barriers to the true self. For what was happening between us mattered. It mattered a lot.

I reached out and touched Ice's shoulder. The tunic was silky and cool beneath my fingers. I smoothed a trail down his arm, over the shining cloth. His eyelids shivered. He blinked once.

The planes of his face were angular, but the skin looked soft. He had no facial hair. Some elves had it, some didn't.

I felt my own five o'clock shadow like a dark roughness on my chin and jaw and I had the fleeting thought: *Would he want me to shave before I kiss him?*

Instead, the thought left me as if it never existed, and I could not resist lifting my hand from his arm and cupping his smooth cheek. I leaned in automatically, desire flaring, and lightly trailed my lips over his. Then I kissed him, chaste and warm, no movement, just our lips pressed together for many seconds.

I could feel that he was not breathing. *Just one more blissful moment*, I thought. I did not want our first kiss to end.

Finally, I leaned back and looked at him; my lips tingled, my chest warmed—my body shuddered in sweet arousal.

Ice was not smiling, but his lips were slightly parted, dampness shimmering along the contours of his mouth.

He was not unaffected, even if he didn't readily show it in his face. His tunic had ridden up. Our bodies were not touching yet, and I could see the outline of his erection in his dark leggings. That was the major sign. But there were other signs. Now that he was breathing again, I heard the shallowness and quickness of it. His fingers squeezed tight over mine.

Outside, the wind suddenly softened to a croon.

Ice abruptly sat up, long hair falling forward, bells ringing. Our hands parted.

"What?" I whispered.

The air became still. I heard his breaths and my own. My heart raced.

"If the world stopped right now," he began. He said nothing further.

I started to sit up, too, but at that very moment he turned, looking me up and down. He paused at my green briefs, noted how I was straining against them. My body gave a slight shudder. Suddenly a little shy, I glanced down, then up. His gaze traveled further down, then his head nodded toward me and our eyes met. He rose on his hands and knees and before I realized it, he was over me, the ends of his hair trailing my arms and alongside my head, his face overhead moving closer and closer to mine.

His lips grazed my jaw and cheek, sending more thrills through my body. Soft and warm, they found their way to my mouth. Slowly, he lowered his upper weight onto me, still holding his lower body away, and danced his tongue into the parting of my mouth.

I opened to him. There was nothing else to do. I could not resist. One hand came up to rest in my hair, the fingers combing through it, lightly touching my scalp.

I shivered.

He pulled back. "Are you cold?"

I shook my head and leaned up into him, begging for a return of that kiss. How could I be cold? The room's temperature had risen to the level of summer.

My arms came around him, hugging.

He groaned aloud, and our lips met again.

I lost time in that kiss, plunged into the depths of bliss, surrounded by electric ardency, by the being who was Ice, and who I now wanted with all my soul.

I spread my legs, bare against his leggings, and he gradually rested his weight between them.

His hand strayed from my hair and pressed between us, tugging at my shirt. He kissed me hard, and pulled until I felt a tear, heard a pop.

Slow down, I thought. *I will still love you thirty seconds from now.*

But I only chuckled into our kiss, and unclasped my hold on him so I could wrestle my hands between us and undo my own shirt.

Ice took that moment to rise up and pull off his tunic in one fluid move. He tossed it over the edge of the bed.

His skin was hairless and perfect, the muscles defined by his leanness, taught and firm with youth. The ends of his hair teased his sweet, pink nipples, small and erect. His skin tone was pale but infused with a golden tone that made him look carved from sunlight.

I pulled my arms from my white shirt-sleeves and vest, and raised them up to his chest, running them over it and down his sides. Like satin.

"You're lovely." My voice quavered.

He swallowed tightly, placing one palm in the center of my chest. My heart pounded against that small weight which did not move for awhile, as if he was counting. My back met the bed again.

64

He leaned down, his hand moving up to push the hair from my brow. Skin to skin, our new embrace turned quickly molten.

I thrust my brief-clad hips to meet his. I leaned up tighter against him and our arms went around each other. We rolled to our sides, still kissing, some of his hair falling over our faces in a chime. He pushed it back and held his hand against my cheek.

I was first to move my hand into further intimacy, down his back and into the waistband of his tights. I wiggled my fingers beneath the stretch of cloth where his skin grew more rounded and pliant, even softer.

He moaned into my mouth, low and pleasant.

I wanted all the walls down, all the barriers. Instead, I paced myself. Savored.

I moved my lips down over his chin and to his chest, licking and nipping. Over the contours of muscles, onto a nipple, suckling, moving on. Every breath he drew was like a long and held back sigh, as if he was trying to hold onto the last of his heart's coverings.

Ice's own hands were far from idle. They both pressed into my hair now, holding my head as if to guide me. He did not push, though. He caressed. But I wanted him looser, out of control. He always walked through the workshop with such a self-contained presence, body tall and almost regal, stiff, glowering. Everything held back.

I wanted to see him melt and lose himself in euphoria.

Ice. My Ice. This day. This night. He was my whole meaning for now. And for longer, I hoped.

I started to nuzzle his belly and below, and he snarled and pulled me back up, kissing me fiercely.

I spoke into the kiss. "I wasn't done."

"No, you weren't."

I laughed. He pushed me down and started his own exploration of me. Soft lips and strolling fingers. He tasted my skin starting at my neck and moving down. His mouth on my nipples nearly brought me to orgasm. But he gentled his touches, and skimmed and tapped, licked and kissed. Over my ribs and stomach, down and down.

I bent my knees and thrashed my body from side to side. Low sounds escaped my throat. His lips hit the barrier of my elastic waistband, my green briefs with the little white line of fake fur at the waist and thighs. His teeth caught the edge. His hand went down and his thumb caught and lifted, then pushed. The briefs were down my thighs before I realized it, and he pulled them all the way off and threw them aside by way of his tunic.

I lifted my head, watching him take me in, his eyes moving, looking everywhere, his hands rubbing my thighs as if he wanted them open.

I couldn't stop myself from letting my bent knees spread. My cock quivered, hard against my abdomen. One hand brushed under one thigh at the edge of my ass, and briefly grazed my balls.

"Oh gods!"

Ice bent closer but did not repeat the gesture.

If he looked at me long enough, I would come from just his gaze. I felt so vulnerable, literally shuddering inside my skin, wanting release but more. I wanted him to like what he saw, want it, want me.

This was a habit with me around others, this need for outside approval, but mostly in the workplace. In the past, in bed, I'd enjoyed compliments, but I never cared enough to agonize over not getting them. There was a reason for that. I'd never really been in love. I'd only had for-fun sex before. Never much more than that.

But this. This scared me. This moment was important.

I took a deep breath and it sounded like a hiss falling into the air.

Ice looked up at me. Our eyes met. Everything between us was wordless and clear, but still scary, still dark and unknown. His eyes asked me, *Are you okay?*

I nodded once.

Still staring at me, half lying on his side, he stroked over my ribs, down my stomach and gently encased my cock in his hand. He held it lightly, then squeezed. A gentle pressure. A reverent clasp.

The room spun. My eyes stared up at the ceiling where little motes in the air became stars, where universes were beginning to form in this tiny room in a cabin in the middle of the frozen, cold North Pole.

From far away now, I heard him whisper my name. The hand on my cock moved, pulling up, then came the warm laps of tongue, the press of lips.

My hands gripped the bedspread hard. My eyes closed.

The mouth descended on my stiff flesh, sucking.

I became all sensation, all bliss, a rhapsody of its own making. My song, a wish that I could move upon the forever-ness with this deep nearness, this connection to another, this understanding, and never have it leave me.

He drove me from dreamy splendor to serious need in moments. I pressed up. I came hard. The cries that escaped me might have sounded forlorn to just anyone passing by. They were anything but.

He did not let up for awhile, licking, kissing, moving his lips up and down my hard length. That meant he drank it all, my essence, my elation, my newly forming love.

Did he know? Did he realize? I was falling hard. It had started the moment we took our buckets together to the first floor windows and began getting ready for Santa.

Was that only yesterday? So much had happened.

When Ice finally let me go, he ran his hands up my inner thighs as if to comfort me. He stretched alongside me and took me into his arms. I reached back and kissed him, the sweetness of my orgasm still trembling in my veins.

I held onto him tighter, my leg moving over his still clad thigh, hugging him with my whole body. He wrapped his arm about my shoulder with his hand on the back of my neck and held me so our kiss could deepen.

His hardness pressed against my inner thigh. I drew my hand down his ribs, his taut flank, and caressed his abdomen. Pressing my hand beneath the material that clutched him there, my fingers swept over the head of his damp cock.

He jerked in my arms, arching, and I used my body weight to push him onto his back so I could have my way with him. He went easily back, acquiescing to my will, chest heaving.

I sat up halfway, gripping his shaft gently, and used my other hand to divest him of the rest of his clothing.

Now I could really look at him, see his uninhibited beauty. My hands were dark copper against his pale skin. Dark and light mixing, touching. I moved my hand further down to stroke his balls as his legs fell open. My fingertips brushed the edges of his buttocks, sliding underneath him to cup the curving rise of muscle and flesh. So soft.

I leaned down and licked the head of his cock. His hand reached up and gripped hard at my shoulder.

The grip tightened as I took him into my mouth. Salt and spice. Stretched satin texture. Scent of deepness. The luxury of him.

I might have bruises on my shoulder by morning, but in the moment I felt no pain as his grip tightened. Not even my knee bothered me, cooperating nicely as I leaned before his stretched body, bringing him pleasure with my mouth.

He had very little body hair. Spangled gold surrounded his cock like thick sprinkles of glitter. I had one hand on his thigh, the other on his stomach which was heaving and hot to the touch. He was perfect, so strong and lean.

His breathing quickened. Hand now kneading my shoulder, he moaned low and deep. Three times. The throb of his organ in my mouth delighted me.

The ardent cream of him, essence spent in euphoria, I swallowed it all.

I moved up his body and lay my head on his chest. His arm came around me and we both took several minutes to catch our breaths and bask.

After awhile, and much to my disappointment, he moved out from underneath me and sat up. But his hand lingered on my thigh even as he slid from the bed. Finally, his touch slid away and he headed naked to the bathroom, his loveliness filling me up as if he were air to my suffocating being.

After he returned, I got up myself, knowing he watched me, knowing by how he watched that he was going to welcome me back into his arms. And indeed he did.

We did not need to speak. Everything happening was deeper than mundane, rational understanding. Unfathomable by mere words alone.

The second time we made love, I opened my body for him and everything became liquid undulations and connections beneath layers of self obliterating into the self.

He thrust in and out of me in a way that had me groaning, begging. I made noises that sounded like weeping, and he pushed harder, taking me gently into his arms as he came. Then staying inside me, he stroked me until I came seconds later, body heaving. He held me tight, my back to his chest, and said my name over and over into my ear.

Pumpkin had told me Ice liked me. How could I ever have disbelieved?

When Ice softened and our bodies disconnected, it felt like loss, and yet he held me tighter, rocking me. We lay down and I turned to face him.

I could see in his eyes he was as amazed as I.

"May I stay the night?" My voice came out rough and wet.

Eyes locked, our foreheads met. "Stay," he said, "for as long as you like." A small smile lit his face. "A night. A day. A month. A year." That last phrase was whispered. He frowned a little, eyes closing. "Did I speak too soon?"

His question made him even more endearing. "No."

My leg wove between his. My arm circled his waist. I bent my head and pressed my face to the side of his neck, inhaling him, taking everything I could of him into me.

"I'll stay," I whispered into his skin.

He pulled me tight within his own arms. As I closed my eyes, I felt him pull the blankets up and over us.

The long, long nights were coming. Now I had someone to share them with.

Epilog

The blizzard left behind unyielding cold and a changed landscape of curled ice drifts.

The next morning we made love again, sweetly, slowly, until my skin felt transformed to pure energy. Later, Ice loaned me clothing and a parka. We returned to the workshop.

Our fairy and snowman were gone, back to being a billion scattered ice crystals. But if we wanted to, we could build them again.

When we entered the workshop, we were holding hands, but no one seemed to notice.

Reluctantly, we parted to go to our separate stations in different rooms.

I admit that I did not get much work done that day. As I daydreamed with my paintbrushes poised motionless over the faces of dolls waiting for personalities, Pumpkin came up behind me and patted my back. "Told you he liked you. I'm glad."

Blinking up at him, I said, "Thank you."

Beyond that day, and into late fall, our routine went on the same as we got ready for Christmas Eve. The only difference was I had moved into Ice's cabin. We didn't get much sleep in those weeks, and were often late for work, but everyone understood why and never made an issue of it.

The day before Christmas Eve, when things were most frantic, Ice and I finally found time to have a short break for cocoa and toasted cheese. I went to the electronics room to get him, and saw him reading a gilt card spattered with gold paint about the edges, and ribbons and bells gathered at its crease. It looked hand-painted on vellum, not printed. It showed a snowy scene and a smiling Santa Claus in full red-suited regalia, a sky of stars behind his head.

"Who made that?"

Ice leaned back in his chair, spinning back and forth. He frowned up at me. "Santa."

Santa sent us all Christmas cards, but they had arrived days ago. They were pretty, but stamped. The words and signature inside were mass printed. This one was thick and old-looking. The inside almost looked burnt the parchment was so dark. From where I stood, I could see fancy, curlicue writing hand-done in black ink. I could not see what the writing said, but at the bottom I saw the florid and tantalizing signature of Santa himself. Not a stamp. The real thing!

My body got hot. I bounced a little on my toes, unable to keep still. It looked like it smelled of gingerbread. I wanted to touch it.

"That's not the Christmas card he sent you," I said, trying not to feel jealous. This card was gorgeous. Why did Ice receive it?

"No. This is an invitation."

"An invitation?"

"To Christmas dinner at the castle."

My heart fell. I had wondered about Ice and Santa off and on, but never asked him to explain, and he never talked about it. We were too busy with other things anyway during our private time to ever talk about Santa. But this was like a blow.

An invitation to the castle at Christmas was unprecedented. After his hard night of work on Christmas Eve, Santa took Christmas Day off. Always.

How could this be? Ice hated Santa. Santa had cancelled Ice's vampire project and shown such disapproval. And now Ice was invited for Christmas dinner?

"Why would you get an invitation like that?"

"It's complicated."

"But you don't even like him. Are—are you going?" My old insecurities slammed me.

"I should."

"Oh." I glanced away, not asking why, bowing my head so he wouldn't see the heat in my eyes.

I had wondered if they had once been lovers. My mind couldn't help but go there again.

Then Ice said, "The invitation's for two. Will you come with me?"

I looked up. "Me? Would Santa even approve?"

His eyebrows narrowed. "Well, I'm allowed to bring anyone I want. So we shall see."

"Well, yes, of course I want to go." I bounced a little harder, excitement warring with trepidation. A visit to the castle? I might faint before I got there.

"Good."

I leaned closer to Ice, touching his shoulder. "Can I see the card?"

He held it out. I took it reverently, gently as if it might crumble. It did indeed smell sweet and spicy like gingerbread. The weight of it made it into a sort of souvenir, something you might keep forever. Inside, in flowery, handwritten script, I read the salutation.

You are invited:

Christmas Day
Santa's Castle
6 p.m.
Dinner and drinks
Casual attire
Bring a guest

Hohoho

Santa Claus

I held the card to my nose again, inhaling.

"Why did you get this? Is Santa approving your project?"

"No."

"But—but no one goes to the castle on Christmas Day. That's Santa's day of rest."

"Well, Pepper, like I said. We shall see."

"It's so beautiful." I held the card in my palm, blinking at its glimmering beauty. "But I still don't understand. Why you?"

Ice stood from his chair, put his arms around me and kissed me on the cheek. "Gods, I fucking love it when you fret, Pepper."

*

There was no light from the sun, which never rose this time of year. But the castle glowed with candles and lanterns in every peak, window and crevice. Like fairy castles of old.

It really was made of ice. And the stars above it simmered as if in poor reflection of this North Pole majestic architecture that was the home of the great Santa Claus. The door to the ice castle itself was pure oak, with a huge holly wreath framing a doorknocker carved in the shape of a reindeer.

Ice and I approached. Despite the invitation's statement for casual attire, we wore our best suits, striped red and white vests, and long sweaters underneath our dark, woolen cloaks. Our hats trailed their points at our shoulders. Ice lifted his hand. I expected him to use the knocker, but instead he grasped the door's handle, flicked the button and entered without announcement. It was so like Ice to do this, brazen and bold.

I'd been to the castle only once. To meet Santa and be accepted as a worker in Santa's Village. It seemed so long ago.

The foyer was cool and white and empty, except for hooks shaped like reindeer antlers where we hung our cloaks and parkas. It led to a huge bustling front room filled floor-to-ceiling with Christmas decorations. Every surface was covered with red or green cloths, topped with sculptures of Santa Claus from around the human world and every culture. Interspersed were snowmen, dolls in Santa suits, snow globes, and candelabras with green and red candles, all lit. A hearth fire flickered and spit with joy. Pine boughs decorated the mantel along with colorful woven stockings bulging with gifts. A massive pine tree laden with ornaments of all colors shaped like orbs, icicles, teardrops and snowflakes stood in one corner. All manner of scents filled the room: roast turkey, apple pie, pine, myrrh, mint.

Just then, Santa came in from another room, golden light at his back. He still had his full white beard from Christmas Eve, but he was dressed in a green suit and he looked thinner than the last time I'd seen him. That was normal. Christmas Eve took a lot out of him despite all the cookies and cakes he ate during his gift-delivering journey.

Just the sight of him made me start to bounce on my toes. But he did not look at me. He looked at Ice.

"Hello, son, I'm glad you could make it. I knew you were mad at me for canceling your project, but you can never stay angry at me for long, can you?"

Son? Of course. It made so much sense to me now. Ice was Santa's son. My body trembled in exhilaration at the information.

Ice let a faint smile show, still so utterly calm. But it was enough for his father to respond. Santa held out his arms and Ice went to him and accepted the hug of father to son.

What a secret to keep, though. And for all this time! But I understood why. Ice had always wanted to do his own thing. His legacy had haunted him possibly more than I could ever know.

Santa turned to me. I caught my breath at his grandeur.

"Merry Christmas, sir," I said, my voice more faint than I would have liked.

"I'm so glad you could make it as well." Santa smiled with all the charm an elf of his magnificence could manifest, and I was struck dumb. He came forward then, and embraced me, his big arms and his warmth surrounding me.

"I'm so glad you and Ice found each other," Santa said to me. He stepped back, his hands still touching my shoulders.

I glanced over to Ice, not even bothering to hide that I was grinning from ear to pointed ear. He crossed his arms over his chest and nodded once at me, winking, his hair chiming with the new bells I had braided into it hours ago. I was so in love with him, I could only stand there, frozen in astonishment.

Santa must've seen the look on my face for what it represented. Love. Pure and absolute.

"Merry Christmas, Pepper," he said. "Welcome to the family."

Dear Reader:

Thank you for reading my cozy Christmas romance.

If you enjoyed this, you might also enjoy subscribing to my newsletter. I put it out about six times a year to announce new books and upcoming projects, and I always have sales and freebies to offer readers both from myself and other authors I enjoy reading. If you subscribe at the link below, you can get a free copy of my book "Letters to an Android".

Happy Holidays!
Wendy Rathbone

Contact links for Wendy:

Facebook: https://www.facebook.com/wendy.rathbone.3

Blog: http://wendyrathbone.blogspot.com/

Newsletter sign up (you get a free copy of "Letters to an Android"):
https://www.instafreebie.com/free/3ErH0

About Wendy Rathbone

I love to write. I have this thing about words and how they are used to describe beauty, love, and all the things that open us up inside to our true self, our power. Words do that for me. They make me happy. The new moon smiling, the sadness of a fallen feather at dusk, predatory eyes gazing through smoke.

The reason I write romance these days is because the overwhelming power of falling in love (which has been proven to heal even cancer) is a game-changer. It makes sad people instantly happy. It makes bleak reality look sun-warmed and friendly again.

I have written in all genres: scifi, fantasy, horror, paranormal, contemporary, erotica, romance. My poetry has won awards, publishing contracts, and was recently nominated for a Pushcart. An early fiction story of mine won Writers of the Future. My fantasy/horror fiction and poetry has received honorable mentions from esteemed editor Ellen Datlow in "Years Best Fantasy and Horror". I am a hybrid writer, publishing both indie (under my press name Eye Scry Designs) and with publishers, most recently with Dreamspinner Press.

I keep coming back to romance. Gay romance. Male/male romance. Maybe it was the wonderful start I got, when I was very young, in Star Trek slash fanfiction. Something about that stuck. And the idea of two men falling in love in a society that has winced at that sort of thing for far too long (when in ancient times and other cultures it is considered normal). The forbidden is imminently appealing and erotic to me. Many of my themes involve abduction, pleasure slavery, indentured servitude, imprisonment. It's like, with my writing, I'm constantly breaking out of some self-imposed cage and letting my wings unfurl until I can finally fly.

This is why I write. This is what makes me burn.

I can give you credentials, lists of awards, books, but in the end for me and hopefully for my readers it comes down to love. Love for writing. Love for reading. Love for romance.

All my books are available on Kindle and Createspace. So if you have the urge, go take a look. See what's on the shelf.

Love to you all!

Wendy Rathbone

LETTERS TO AN ANDROID
Wendy Rathbone

Cobalt is a created human, vat grown and born adult, with no human rights and indentured to serve others for the duration of his life. Liyan is a young man with wanderlust in his eyes, embarking on a career that takes him to the furthest regions of space. The two become unlikely friends and create a memorable long-distance correspondence. Through Liyan, Cobalt gets to explore the universe, living vicariously through his friend's wave transmissions. A strong bond develops between them that not even the stars can put asunder.

―――――――――――――

Now you know an android who writes poetry.
This is all your fault. Did you not read my last wave telling you extracurricular activities for my kind are discouraged? Of course this is harmless and strangely enjoyable and does not necessarily require me to leave the hotel. Pel would not care if I wrote lines of equations or nonsensical juxtaposed words. As long as the act does not bring my mental state into question.
However, in history, poetry is often written by the rebels.
So we can keep this to ourselves.
Let me know about your lieutenant's test.
And to give you peace of mind, I never believed you observed me as anything other than human.
Some people are and always will be hateful bigots. Most people are simply uncomfortable in speaking to "property." And anyway, friendship, like poetry, is also discouraged.

Your friend,
Cobalt

FROM THE AUTHOR:
www.eyescrypublications.com

Also at
Letters To An Android

SCOUNDREL
Wendy Rathbone
A male/male romance

Antares is a willing sex slave, trained in the harems of Anada since the age of 18, and owned by a wealthy master who spoils his slaves. But all that changes when Empire soldiers invade Antares' world and he is taken away from the only life he's ever known.

In a colonized galaxy where starships are as common as houseflies, and a dark Empire seeks to control thousands of civilized worlds, there are those who fall through the cracks and refuse to be conquered, including the pirate, Slate, and his crew.

Out in the darkness of the unknown, among Empire soldiers and scoundrels, will bad fates befall Antares and his fellow captive companions?

Will Slate finally find the love he's been looking for his whole life?

Can Slate and Antares ever see eye to eye?

A male/male romance to end all male/male romances!

FROM THE AUTHOR
www.eyescrypublications.com

PALE ZENITH
Wendy Rathbone
A Science Fiction Novel

On a far-flung "Earth" in a parallel universe, two factions are fighting a decades-long psychic war. Young talented psychics are being temporarily kidnapped from present day Earth, seemingly at random, to serve as part of one side's psychic army. They are put under the control of spychiatrists, mysterious machines with many limbs that have a programmed ability to travel time and space and universes to kidnap and control carefully selected humans. The humans never know they are being used; when their missions are completed they are brought back to their universe through time and placed back in their beds, their memories wiped.

———————————

The shadows wound the tall corridor in muted gold, varnished brown. It seemed as though they were in the bowels of a giant serpent coiled outside time, outside space.

When they left the palace, a familiar sun flourished in a clear, blue sky. But this wasn't their sun. Not Zack's sun. It was an alien star burning within a different galaxy in an all too distant universe. Zack looked up squinting, trying to see if he could peer beyond the sky, beyond the pale of midday and into his own timespace, but there was nothing. Only sunlight. Only the thin atmosphere of an Earth not his own.

His back knotted again. Leo's presence was a gelid space inside his chest, empty. Always before he'd felt a warmth there, a sort of pressure like someone's hand pressed gently to his heart. He'd taken Leo for granted knowing, the way a shadow falls when you block the sun, that he was there around him, inside him: blood, air, salt, brain, soul. They were genetic duplicates, twins, spiritual halves. Without him, Zack knew the first icy tugs of panic.

FROM THE AUTHOR
www.eyescrypublications.com

Also at
Pale Zenith

82

The Foundling
by Wendy Rathbone

Diego is a powerful man with a tragic past. Out on the expansive ocean in his private yacht, he discovers a beautiful and mysterious man adrift on a raft, near death. The bond that forms between them in the aftermath of Alec's rescue is one of fierce passion, though lacking in trust. Can they make it work, or will Alec's amnesia bring forth secrets so disturbing as to tear them apart? A passionately erotic love story of desire and darkness, exquisite and explicit.

I can see his struggle between gratitude and uneasiness. He is buffeted by all things new and strange. He does not know where he is from, who he is or what happened to him. He does not know me. There has not been enough time to transition between strangers and friendship.

This isolation of his is something I can identify with, but it is also a feeling no one can help him with until or unless he gets his own life back. And his memory.

If that doesn't happen, then it will take time for him to build a new life. He is polite to me, even friendly, but even a night together during a storm with his arms wrapped tight around my waist doesn't calm the surge I see inside him, the emptiness, the loss, possibly even panic. That night may have reinforced some trust in me, but so far not enough for him to completely relax.

He seeks me out, though. That's something. He sits by me at dinner when he can have any seat of his choosing. I watch him closely when he does not realize it. At dinner the following night after we had only 'slept' together, and before we go to bed again in separate rooms, I notice everything about him, how he moves, the way the air warms when he is closer to me, the dry sheen of his lips as they part for more air when he is reacting to something, or speaking, or eating.

His hands still shake. Anyone else might not notice because he keeps them clasped into fists at his sides or, while sitting, pressed tight to his lap.

I spend another fretful night alone. I dream restlessly, wild, loud and colorful visions I cannot recall at all as soon as my eyes open. All I know is the dreams leave me unfulfilled, impatient.

www.eyescrypublications.com

83

www.ingramcontent.com/pod-product-compliance
Lightning Source LLC
Chambersburg PA
CBHW020639130626
46552CB00003B/1315